MARVEL

W9-DCJ-302

AVENGERS ASSEMBLE
IN ACTION

Publisher Jim Childs
Vice President, Finance Vandana Patel
Executive Director, Business Development Suzanne Albert
Executive Director, Marketing Services Carol Pittard
Executive Director, Marketing Susan Hettleman
Publishing Director Megan Pearlman
Associate Director of Publicity Courtney Greenhalgh
Assistant General Counsel Simone Procas
Assistant Director, Special Sales Ilene Schreider
Senior Marketing Manager, Sales Marketing Danielle Costa
Senior Manager, Business Development + Partnerships
Nina Fleishman Reed
Senior Production Manager Susan Chodakiewicz
Editor, Children's Books Jonathan White
Associate Prepress Manager Alex Voznesenskiy
Assistant Project Manager Hillary Hirsch

Editorial Director Stephen Koepp
Senior Editor Roe D'Angelo
Copy Chief Rina Bander
Design Manager Anne-Michelle Gallero
Editorial Operations Gina Scauzillo

SPECIAL THANKS TO
Katherine Barnet, Brad Beatson, Jeremy Biloon, Rose
Cirrincione, Assu Etsubneh, Mariana Evans, Christine Font,
David Kahn, Jean Kennedy, Amy Mangus, Kimberly Marshall,
Courtney Mifsud, Nina Mistry, Dave Rozzelle, Matthew
Ryan, Ricardo Santiago, Divyam Shrivastava, Holly Smith,
Adriana Tierno

Produced by **DOWNTOWN BOOKWORKS INC.**
President Julie Merberg
Publisher Patty Brown
Editorial Director Sarah Parvis
Editorial Assistant Sara DiSalvo
Cover and Interior Design Georgia Rucker

Published by Time Home Entertainment Inc.
1271 Avenue of the Americas, 6th floor • New York, NY 10020

ISBN 10: 1-61893-376-0
ISBN 13: 978-1-61893-376-8

We welcome your comments and suggestions about Time Home
Entertainment Books. Please write to us at:
Time Home Entertainment Books
Attention: Book Editors
P.O. Box 11016
Des Moines, IA 50336-1016
If you would like to order any of our hardcover Collector's
Edition books, please call us at 1-800-327-6388, Monday
through Friday, 7 a.m.–8 p.m., or Saturday, 7 a.m.–6 p.m.,
Central Time.

1 QGC 14

marvel.com

© 2014 MARVEL

A TIME FOR HEROES

It's the end of the world!

Sorry, sir. I know that was a bit dramatic. It's just that it can be very hard to get your attention. Your most dangerous enemies have broken free from the S.H.I.E.L.D. tri-carrier and joined forces. Alone, each is a deadly threat. Together they may be unstoppable. Shall I activate the Avengers protocol?

Very good, sir.

Read on to learn which of Earth's mightiest heroes answered your call. I think you'll like what you see. Remember, each page can be cut out and hung up.

Now, who do you want on your team?

ASSEMBLE YOUR TEAM

Choose your team carefully, sir, for the right balance of power, skill, intellect, and instinct will be the key to victory!

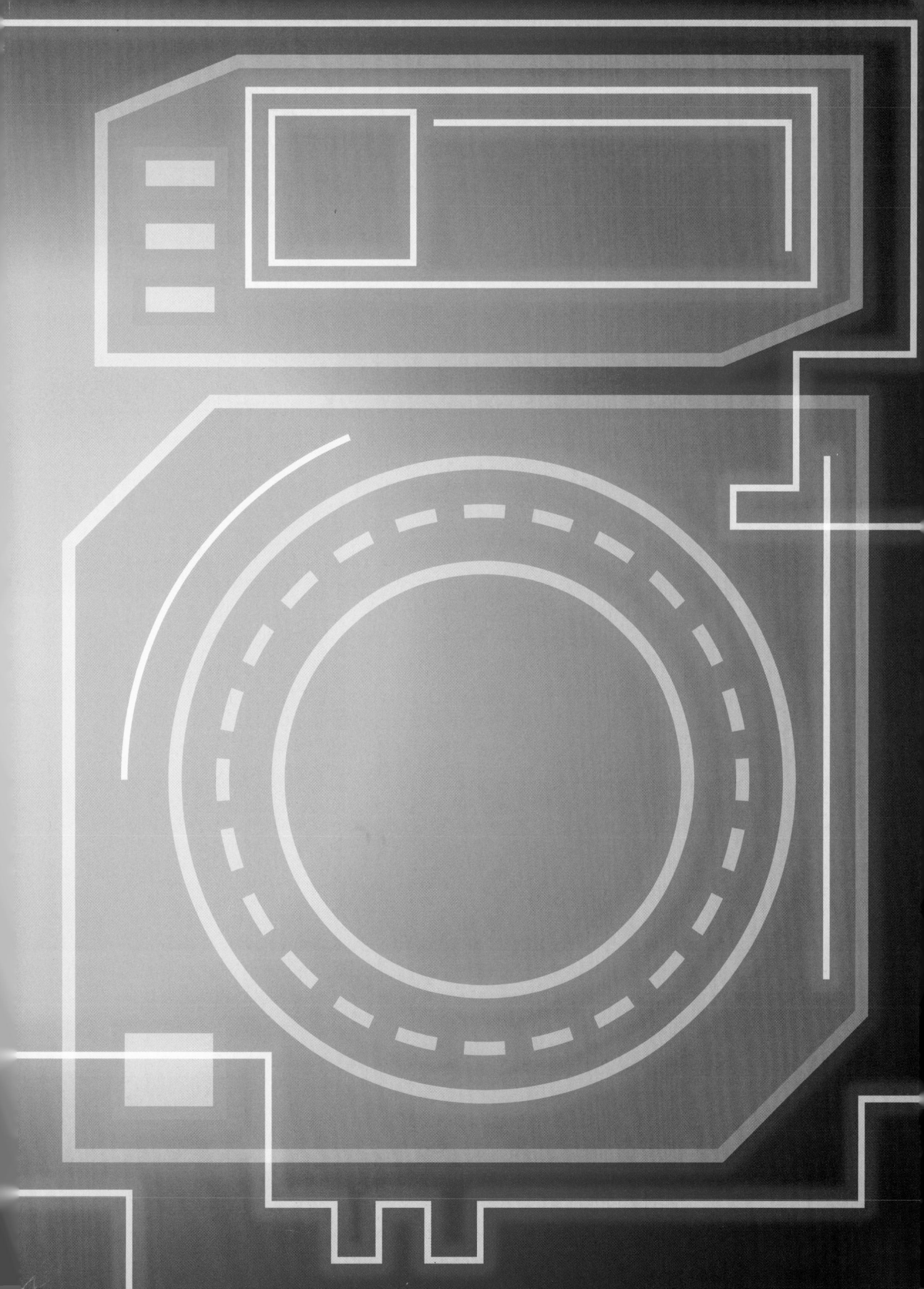

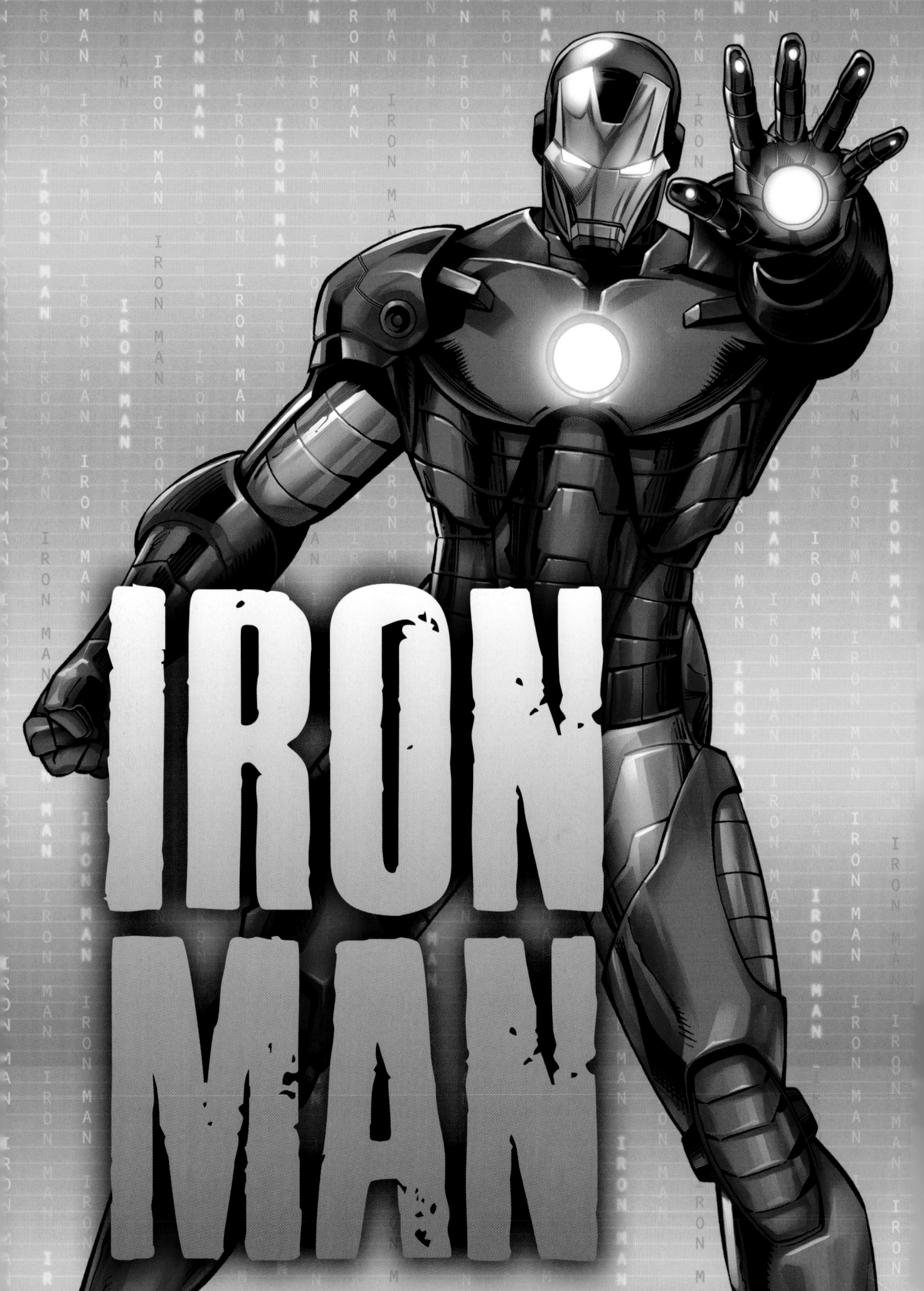

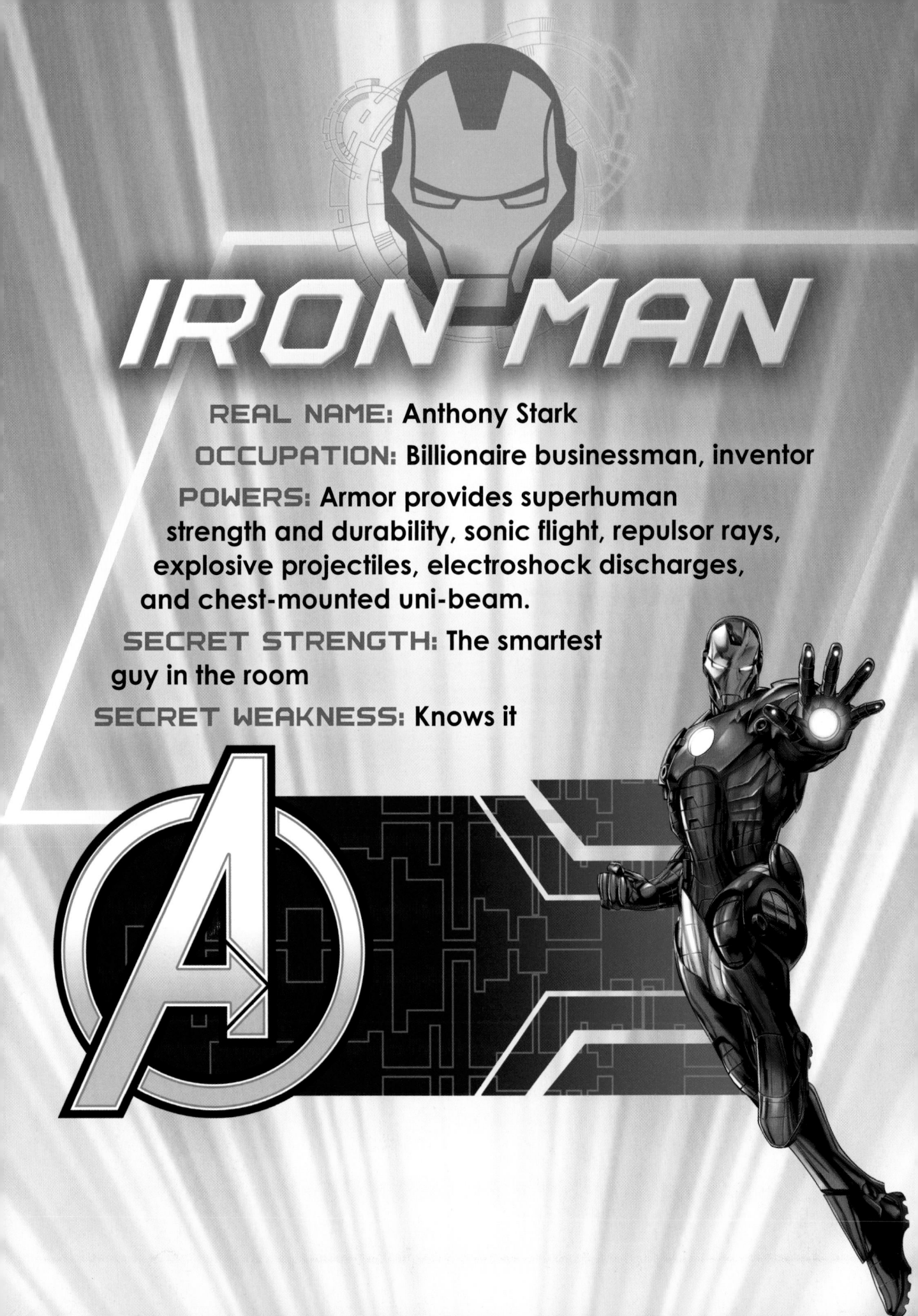

IRON-MAN

REAL NAME: Anthony Stark

OCCUPATION: Billionaire businessman, inventor

POWERS: Armor provides superhuman strength and durability, sonic flight, repulsor rays, explosive projectiles, electroshock discharges, and chest-mounted uni-beam.

SECRET STRENGTH: The smartest guy in the room

SECRET WEAKNESS: Knows it

Joking in the face of certain death is part of my charm.

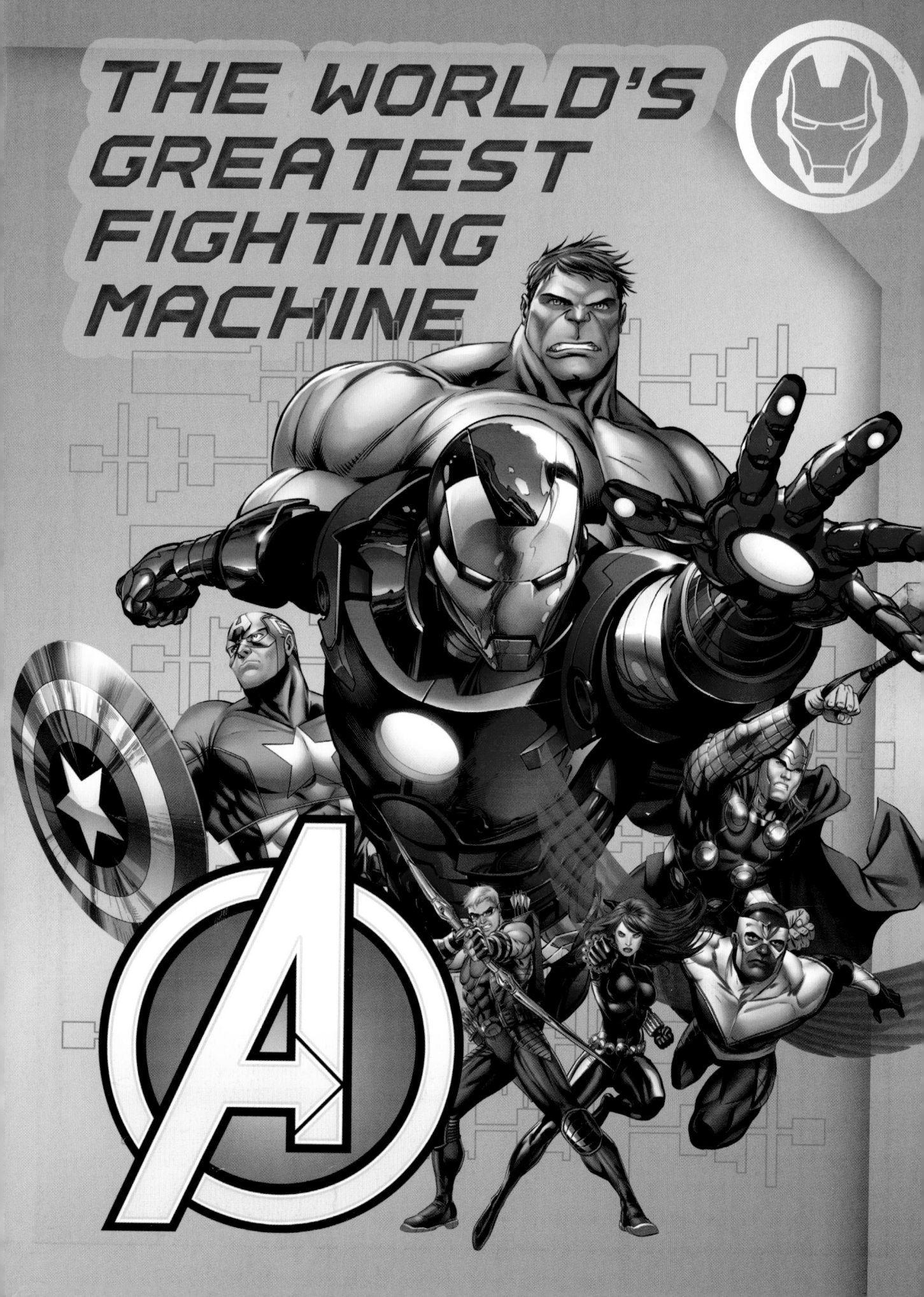

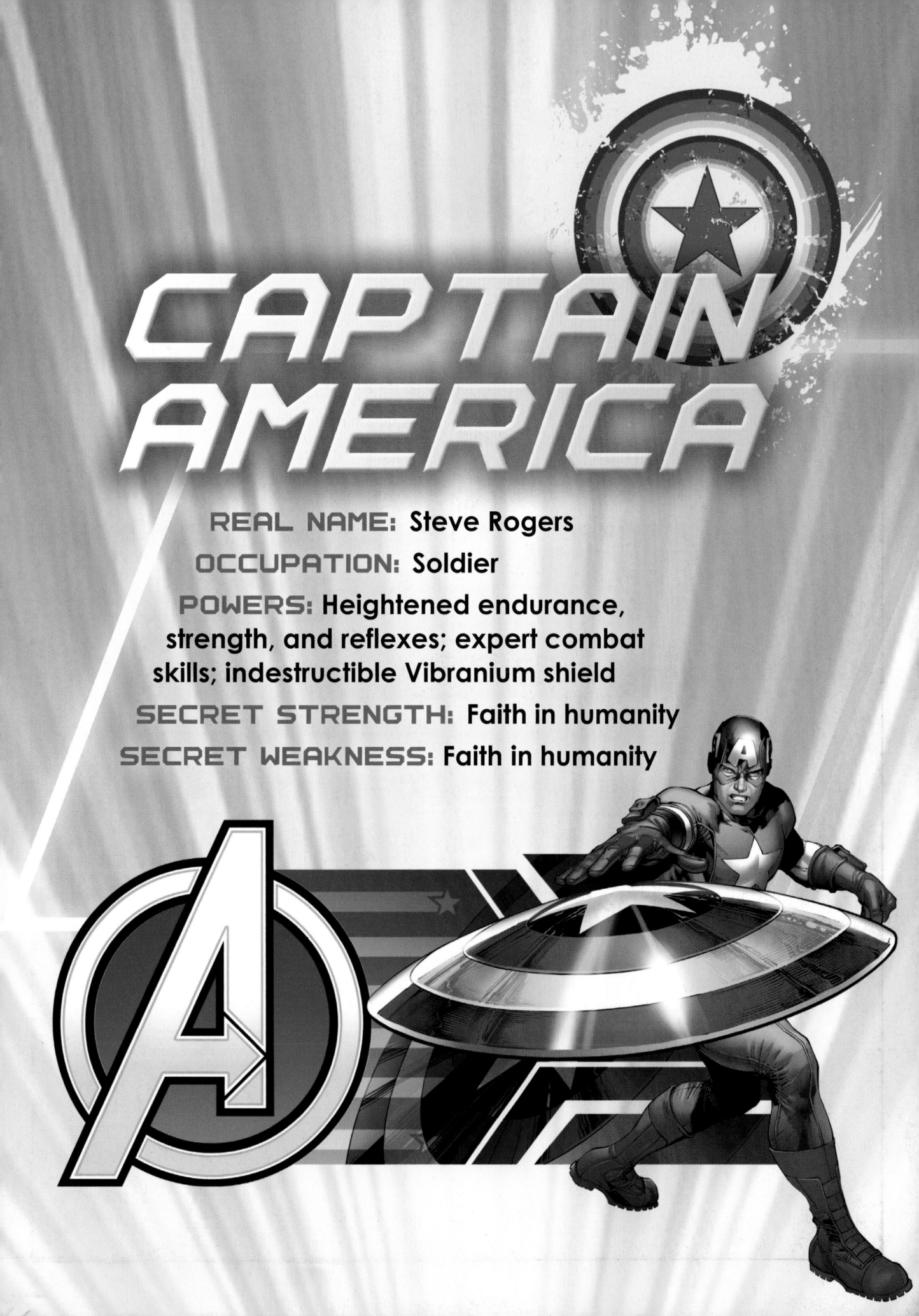

CAPTAIN AMERICA

REAL NAME: Steve Rogers

OCCUPATION: Soldier

POWERS: Heightened endurance, strength, and reflexes; expert combat skills; indestructible Vibranium shield

SECRET STRENGTH: Faith in humanity

SECRET WEAKNESS: Faith in humanity

SENTINEL OF LIBERTY

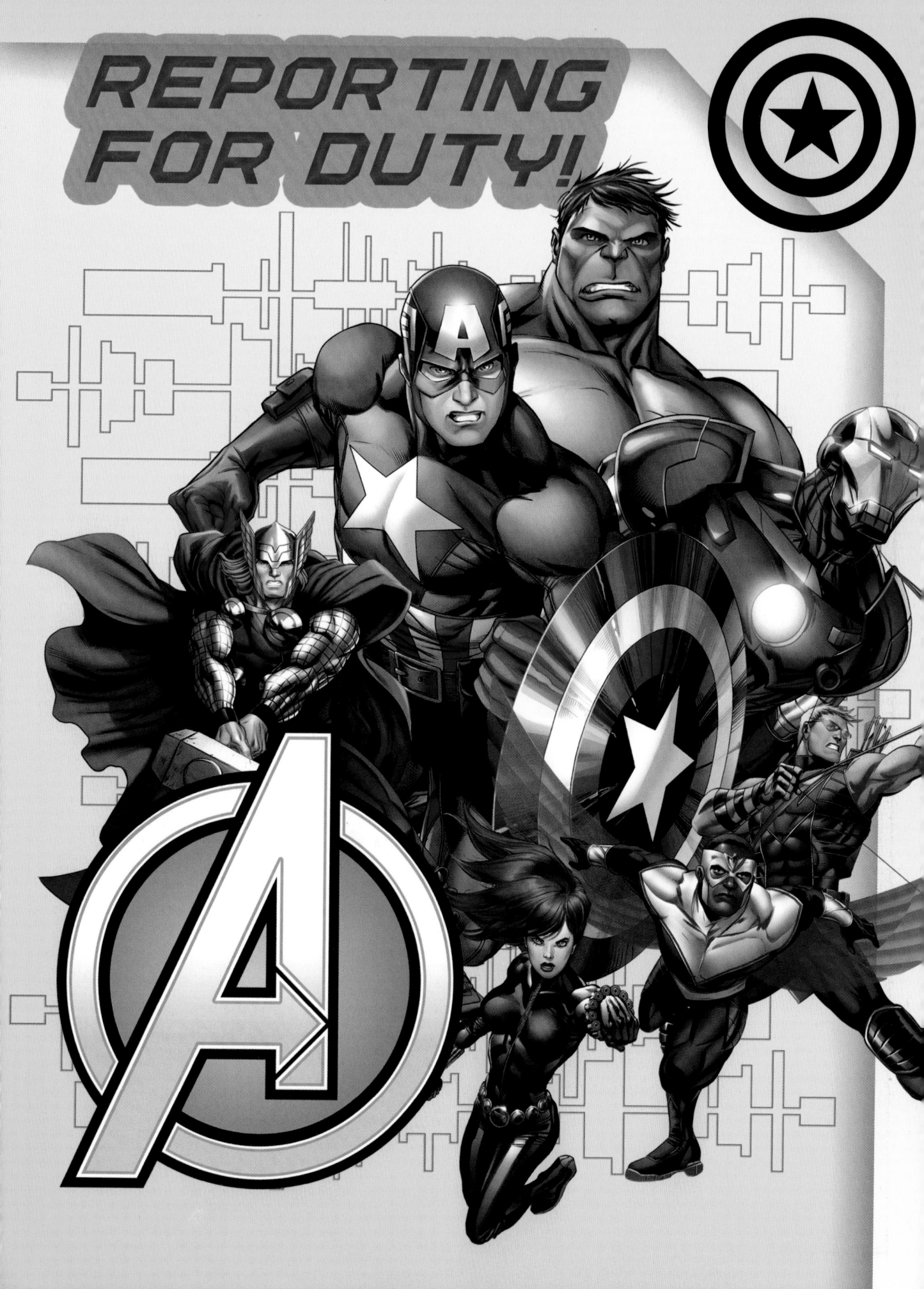

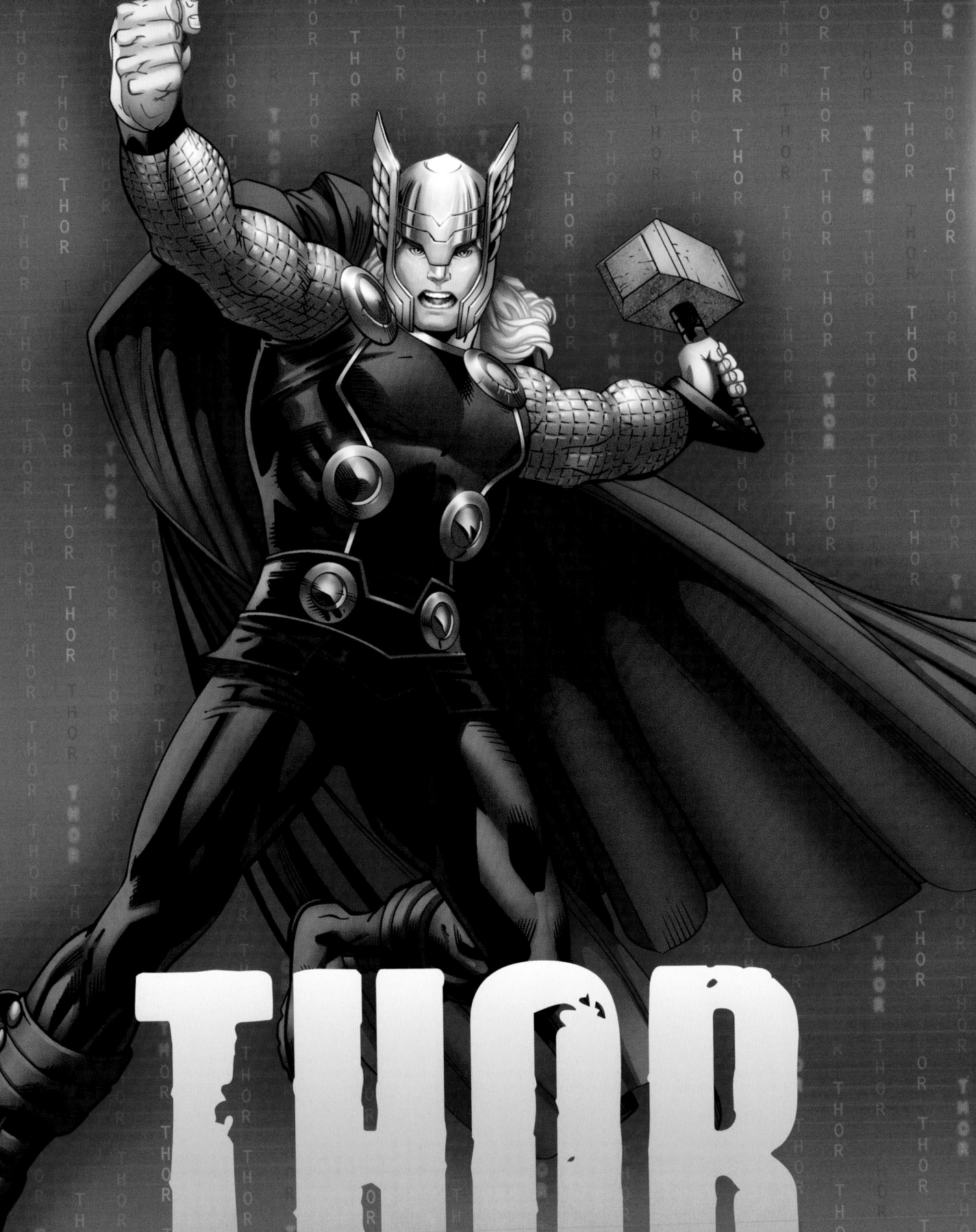

THOR

REAL NAME: Thor Odinson

OCCUPATION: God of Thunder (ret.)

POWERS: Superhuman strength, speed, endurance, and resistance to injury; mastery over thunder and lightning. Hammer adds flight, energy blasts, and ability to open interdimensional gateways.

SECRET STRENGTH: Throws hammer

SECRET WEAKNESS: Loses hammer

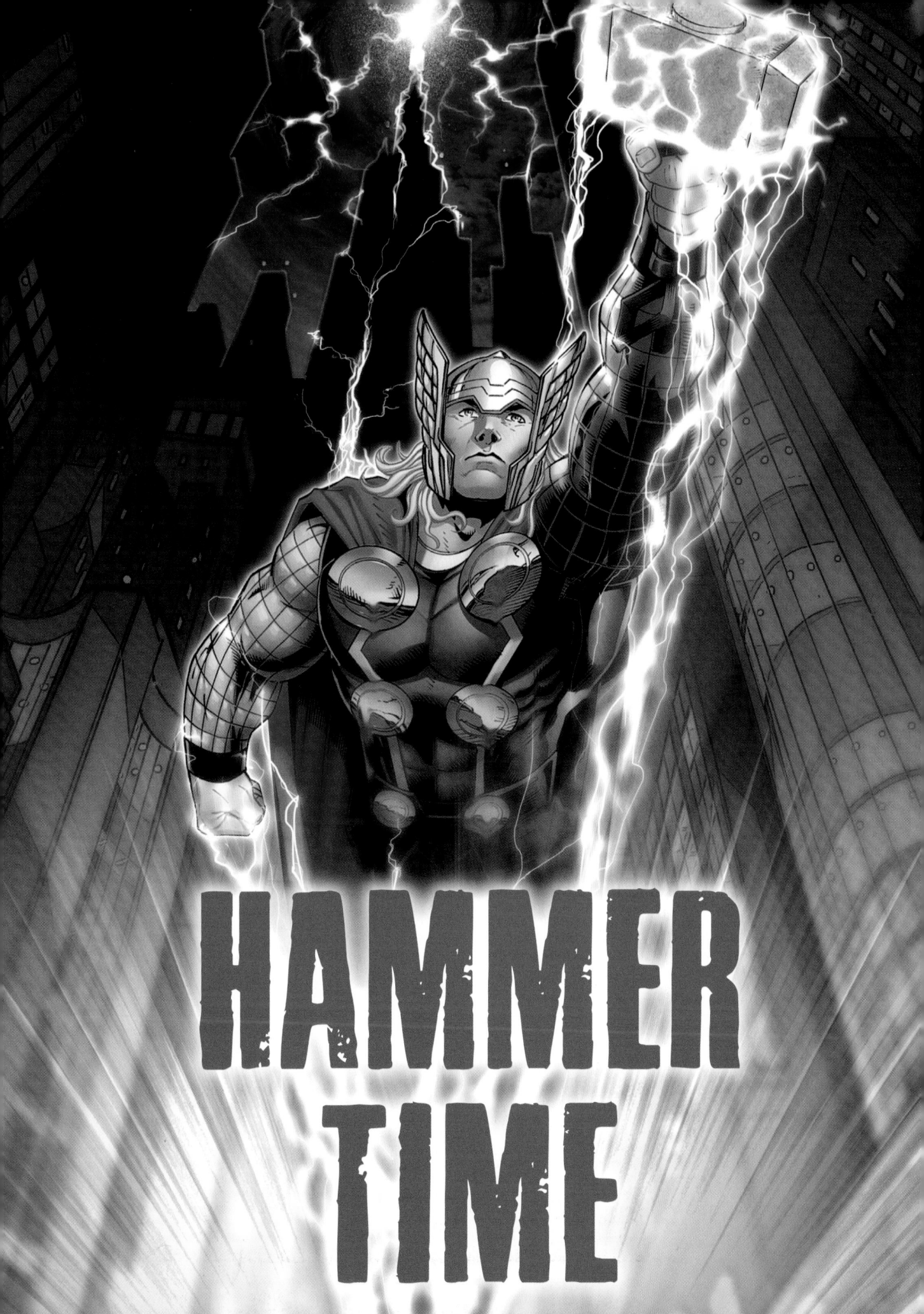

BRING THE THUNDER!

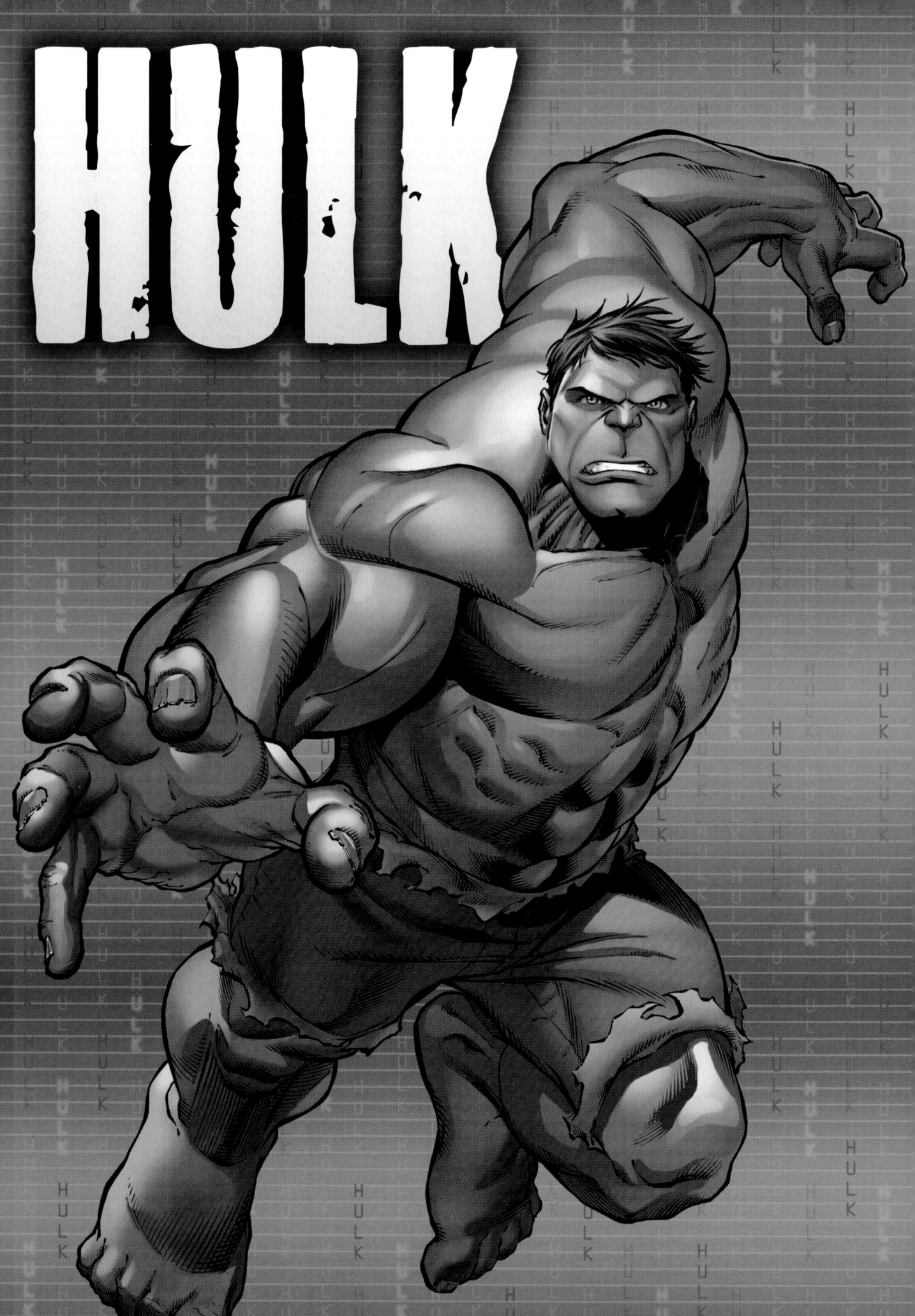

HULK

REAL NAME: Bruce Banner

OCCUPATION: Scientist

POWERS: Incalculable strength, endurance, speed, and healing ability

SECRET STRENGTH: Limitless power

SECRET WEAKNESS: Uncontrollable rage

LESS TALK... MORE SMASH!

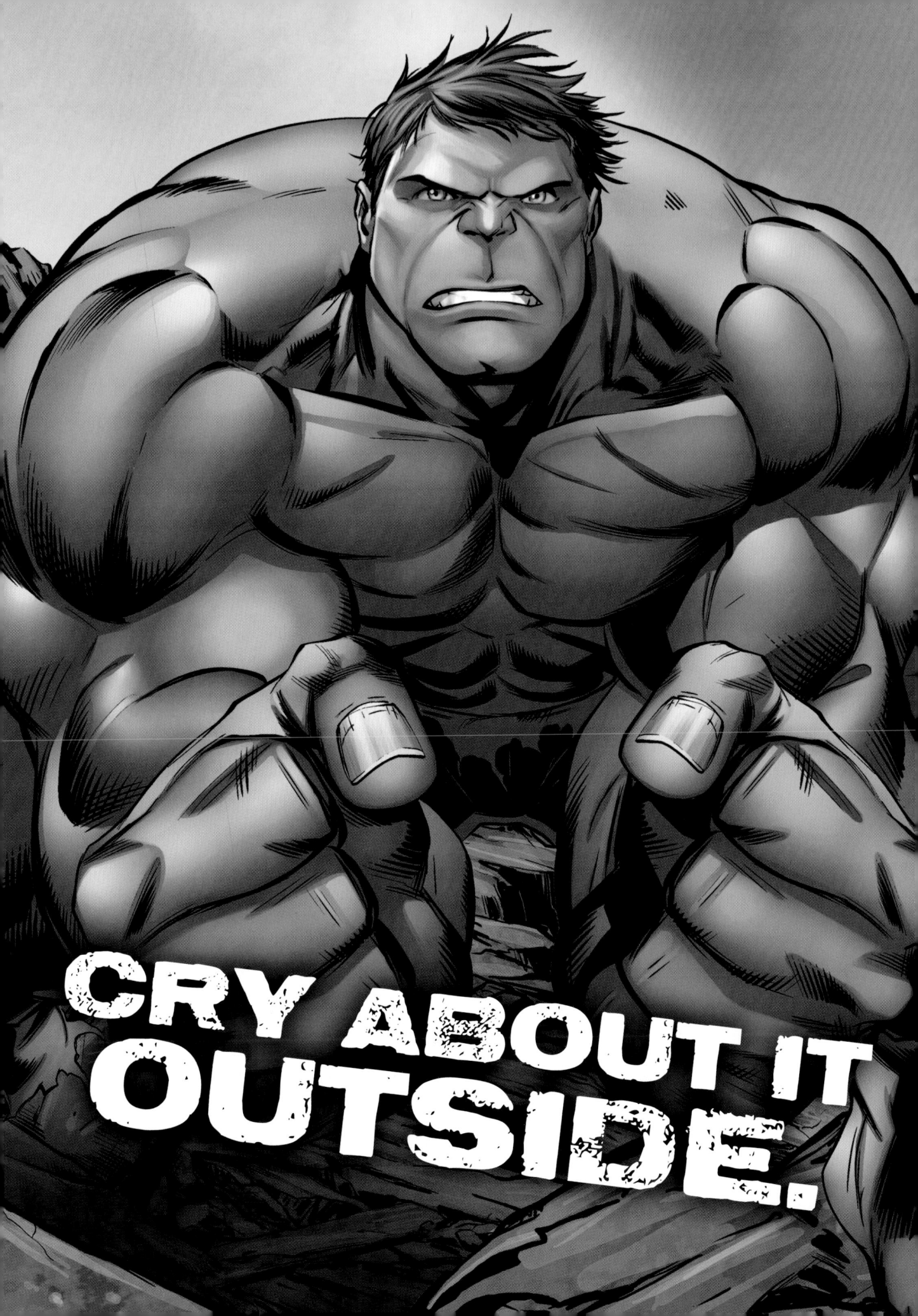

NO COOKIE FOR YOU!

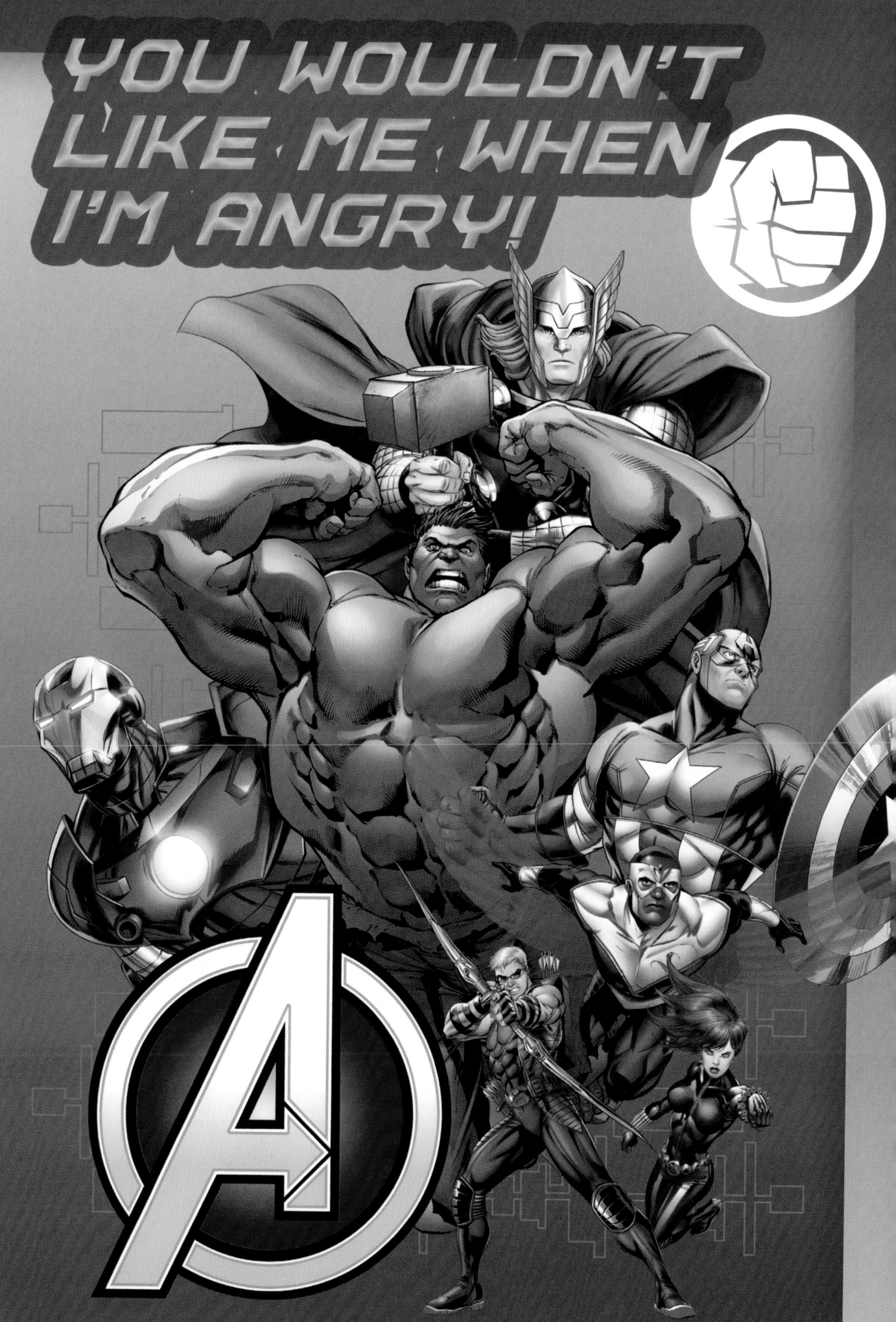

HAWKEYE

REAL NAME: Clint Barton

OCCUPATION: S.H.I.E.L.D. agent

POWERS: World's best archer; expert acrobat and hand-to-hand combatant; custom-made bow and trick arrows

SECRET STRENGTH: Understands the mind of a criminal

SECRET WEAKNESS: Used to be one

I CAN TAKE A MISSION **UN-SERIOUSLY** AND **STILL** ACE IT!

LOCKED ON TARGET

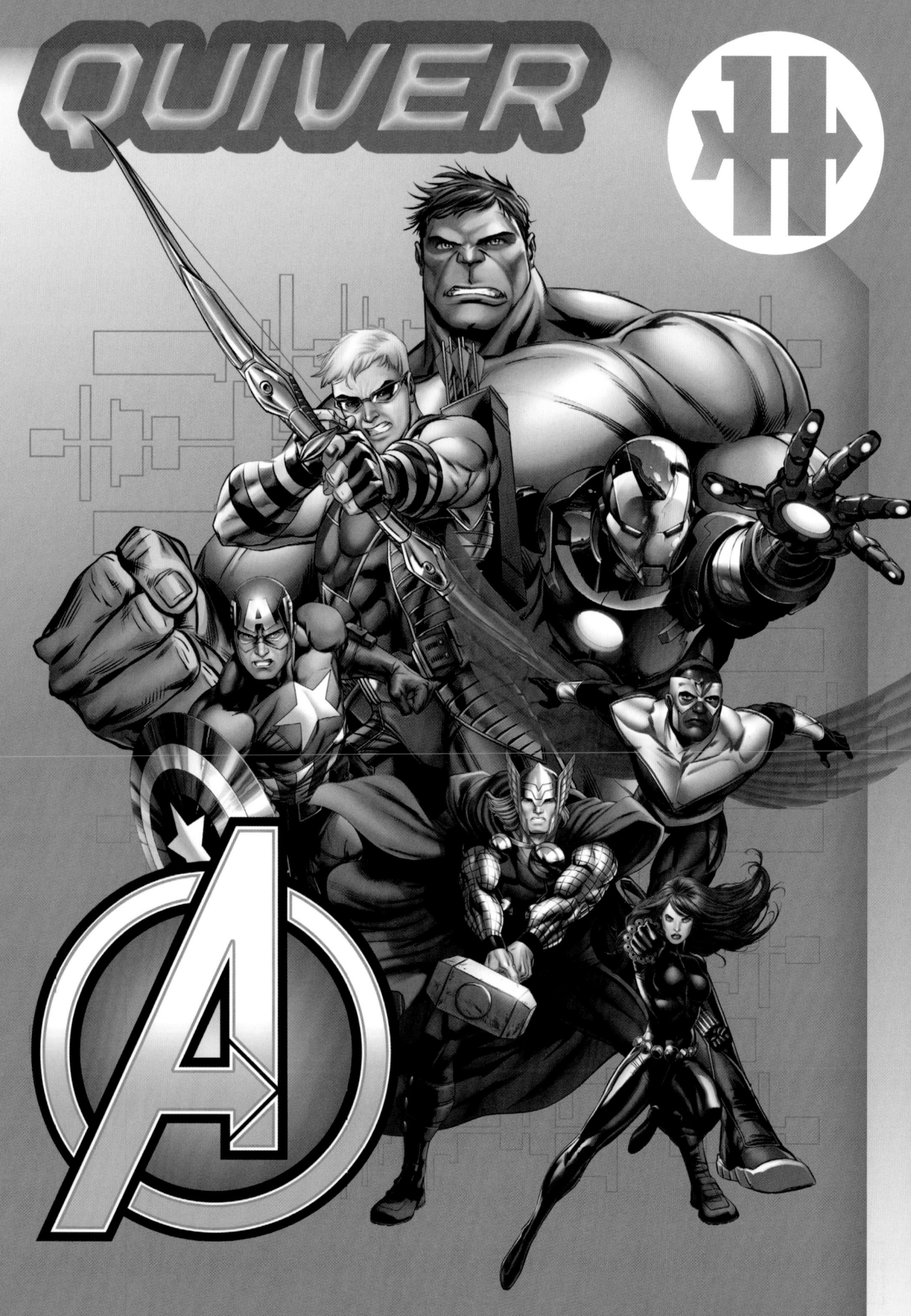

QUIVER

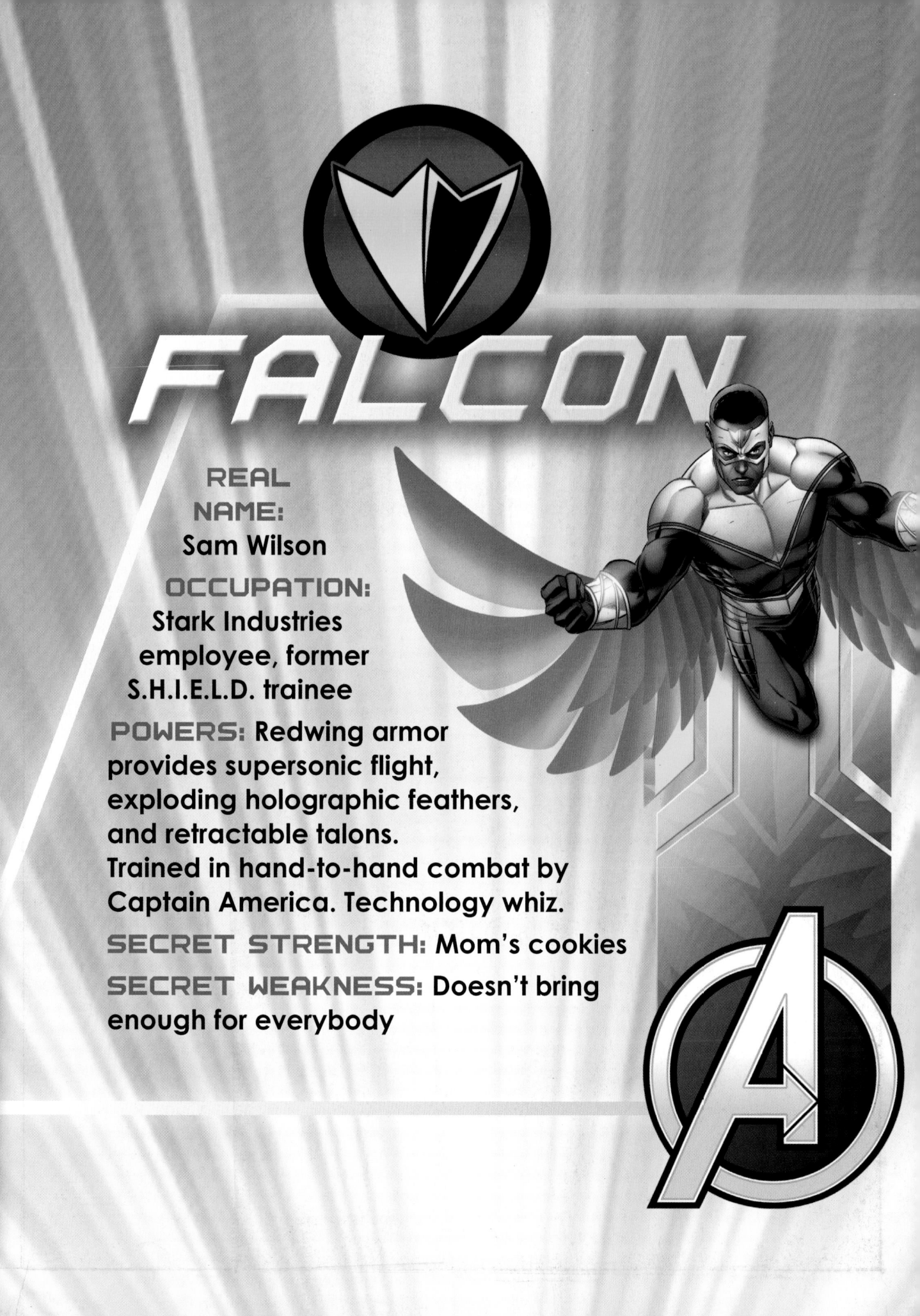

FALCON

REAL NAME: Sam Wilson

OCCUPATION: Stark Industries employee, former S.H.I.E.L.D. trainee

POWERS: Redwing armor provides supersonic flight, exploding holographic feathers, and retractable talons.
Trained in hand-to-hand combat by Captain America. Technology whiz.

SECRET STRENGTH: Mom's cookies

SECRET WEAKNESS: Doesn't bring enough for everybody

THE WINGED AVENGER

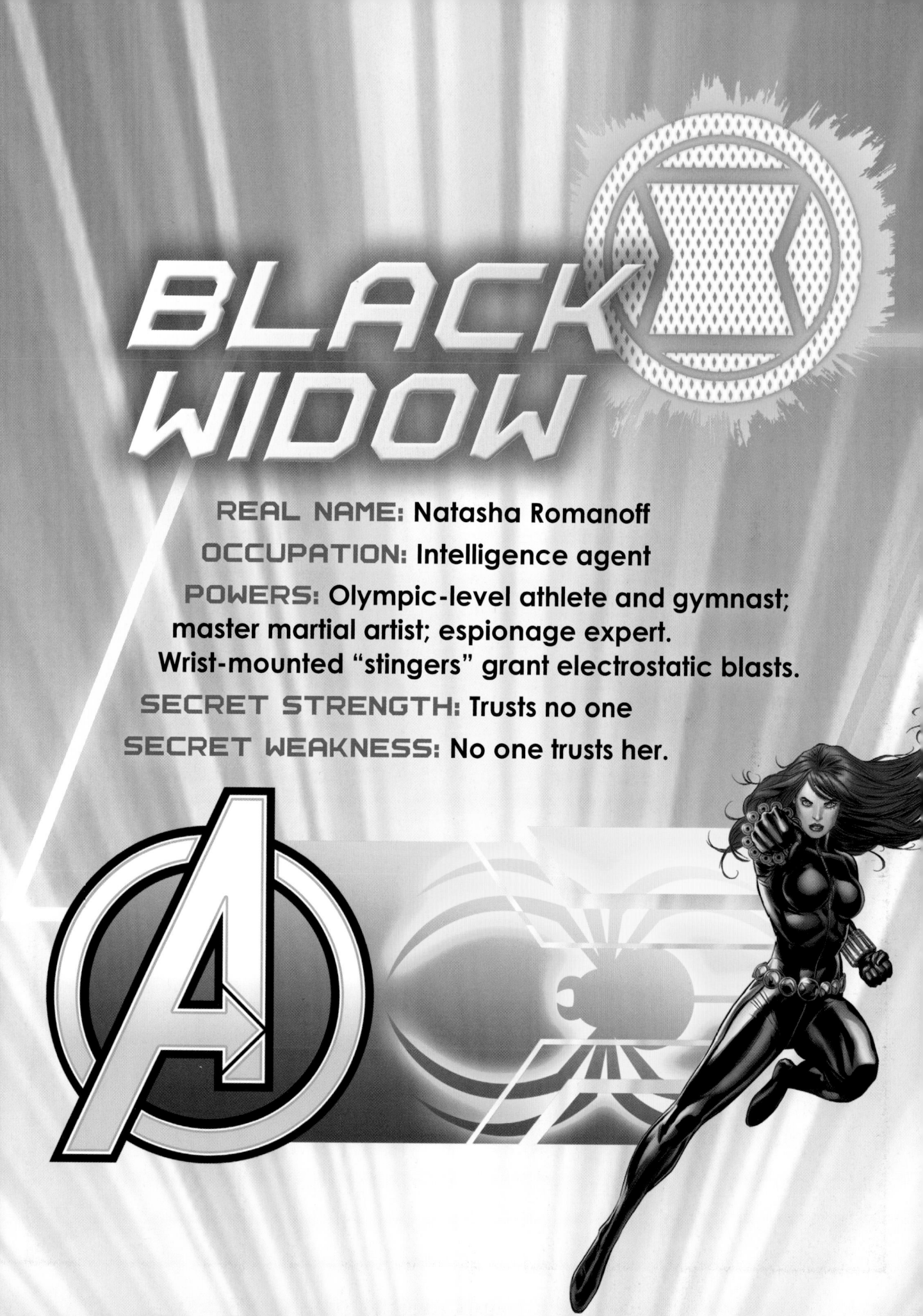

BLACK WIDOW

REAL NAME: Natasha Romanoff

OCCUPATION: Intelligence agent

POWERS: Olympic-level athlete and gymnast; master martial artist; espionage expert. Wrist-mounted "stingers" grant electrostatic blasts.

SECRET STRENGTH: Trusts no one

SECRET WEAKNESS: No one trusts her.

IMPRESSED?
OF COURSE YOU ARE.

SUPER SPY

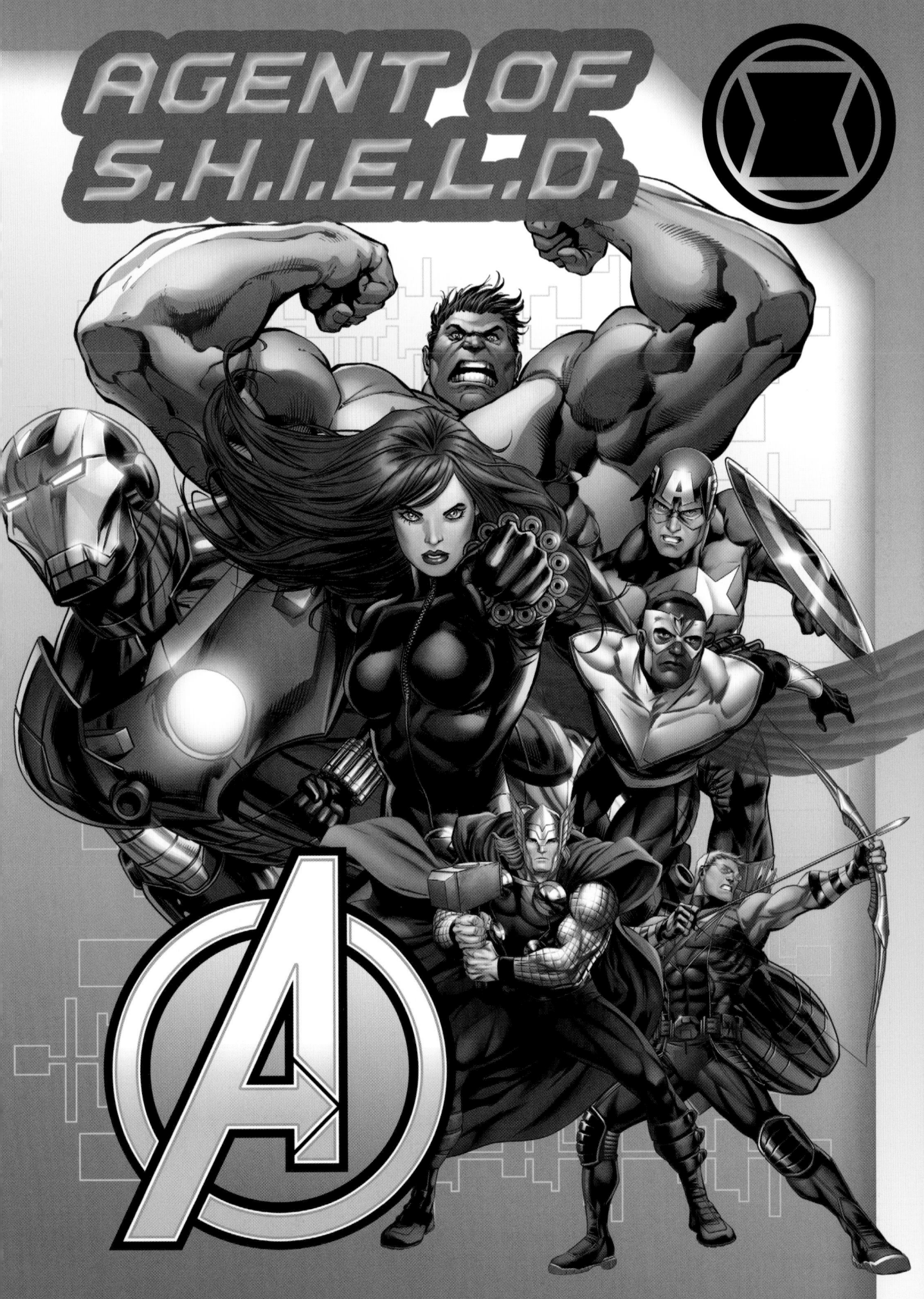

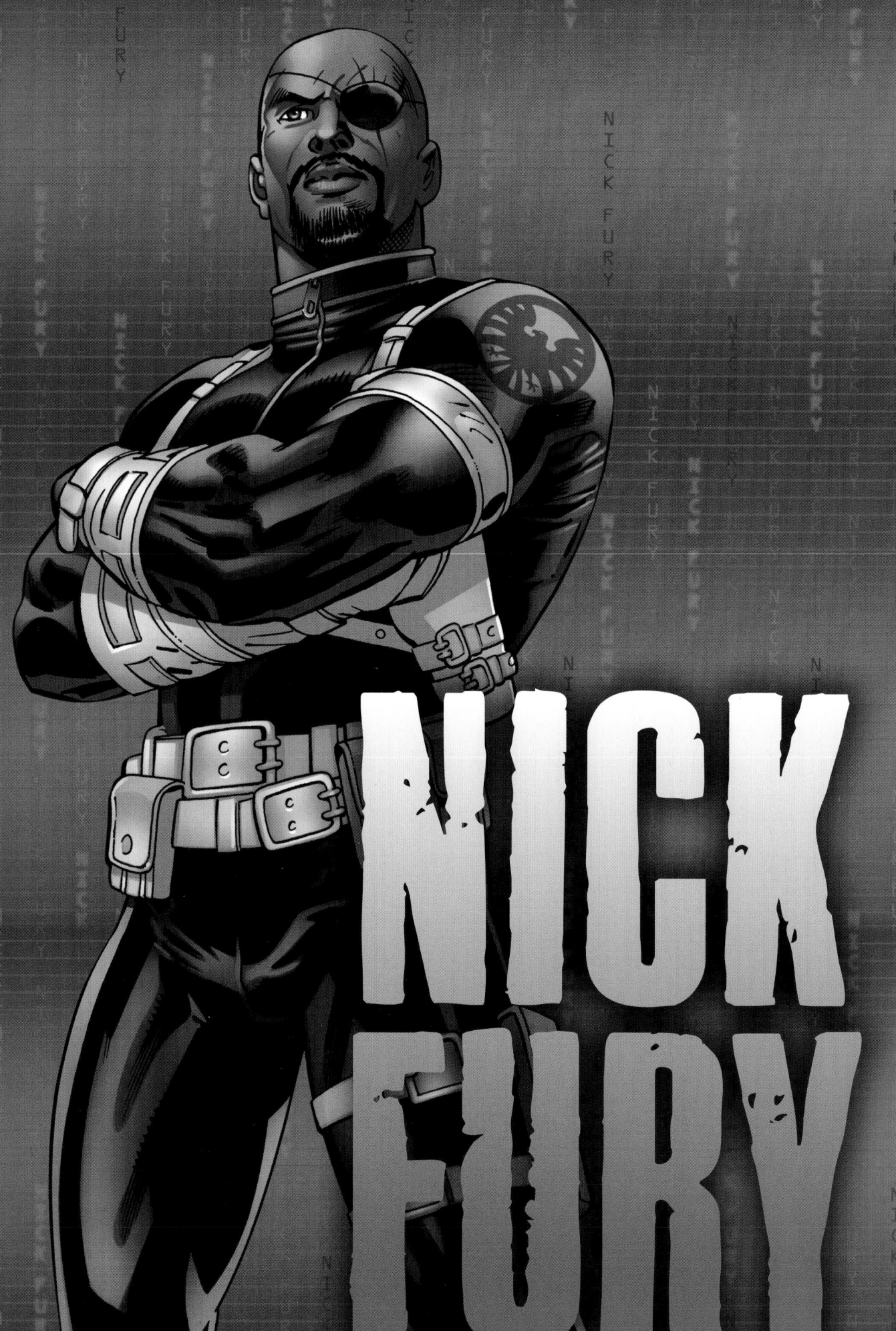

NICK FURY

REAL NAME: Nicholas Joseph Fury

OCCUPATION: Director of S.H.I.E.L.D.

POWERS: Comprehensive military training; expert unarmed and armed combatant; access to and proficiency with entire S.H.I.E.L.D. arsenal of advanced weaponry

SECRET STRENGTH: CLASSIFIED

SECRET WEAKNESS: CLASSIFIED

THE DIRECTOR

I BELIEVE IN SECOND CHANCES.

ARMOR UP:
FROM SHIELD TO S.H.I.E.L.D.

Please put down that arrow, sir. It's full of knockout gas. Perhaps now would be a good time to study your teammates' weaponry? Even an extraordinary intellect such as yours has its limits.

Am I being snarky?

No, sir. You programmed me with no such capacity.

THE MARK 50

More efficient. More powerful. The Mark 50 leaves Tony Stark's old ARC reactor suits in the dust.

THE ARMORED AVENGER

With shoulder-mounted mini missiles and rocket launchers hidden all over it, the Mark 50 makes Iron Man invincible.

REPULSOR TECH:
ARMED AND AIRBORNE

HAND
REPULSORS

BOOT
REPULSORS

IRON MAN'S UNI-BEAM

CONCENTRATED POWER

Electroshock exit-charges zap villains who get too close. When the Mark 50 lights up, it's lights out for evildoers!

Uru metal and Odin's enchantment make mighty Mjolnir the ultimate weapon.

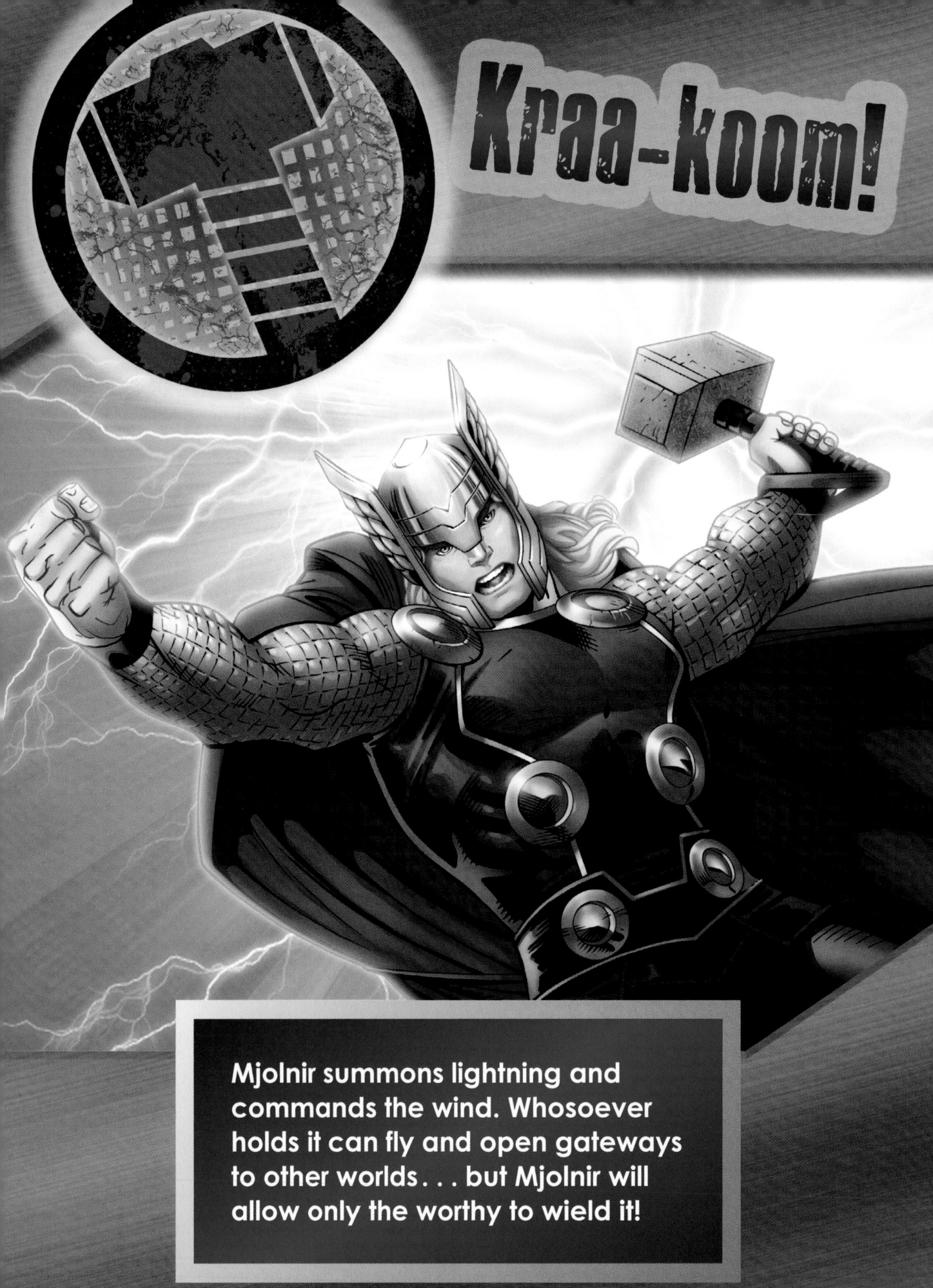

WHOSOEVER HOLDS THIS HAMMER, IF HE BE WORTHY, SHALL POSSESS THE POWER OF THOR!

ARE YOU WORTHY?

THE SHIELD

Rare Vibranium ore makes Cap's shield as indestructible as its owner's spirit.

Super Soldier

Able to absorb or deflect anything from Dr. Doom's energy beams to the Hulk's best punch, Captain America's shield is often thrown with unerring aim. When the shield flies, villains see stars.

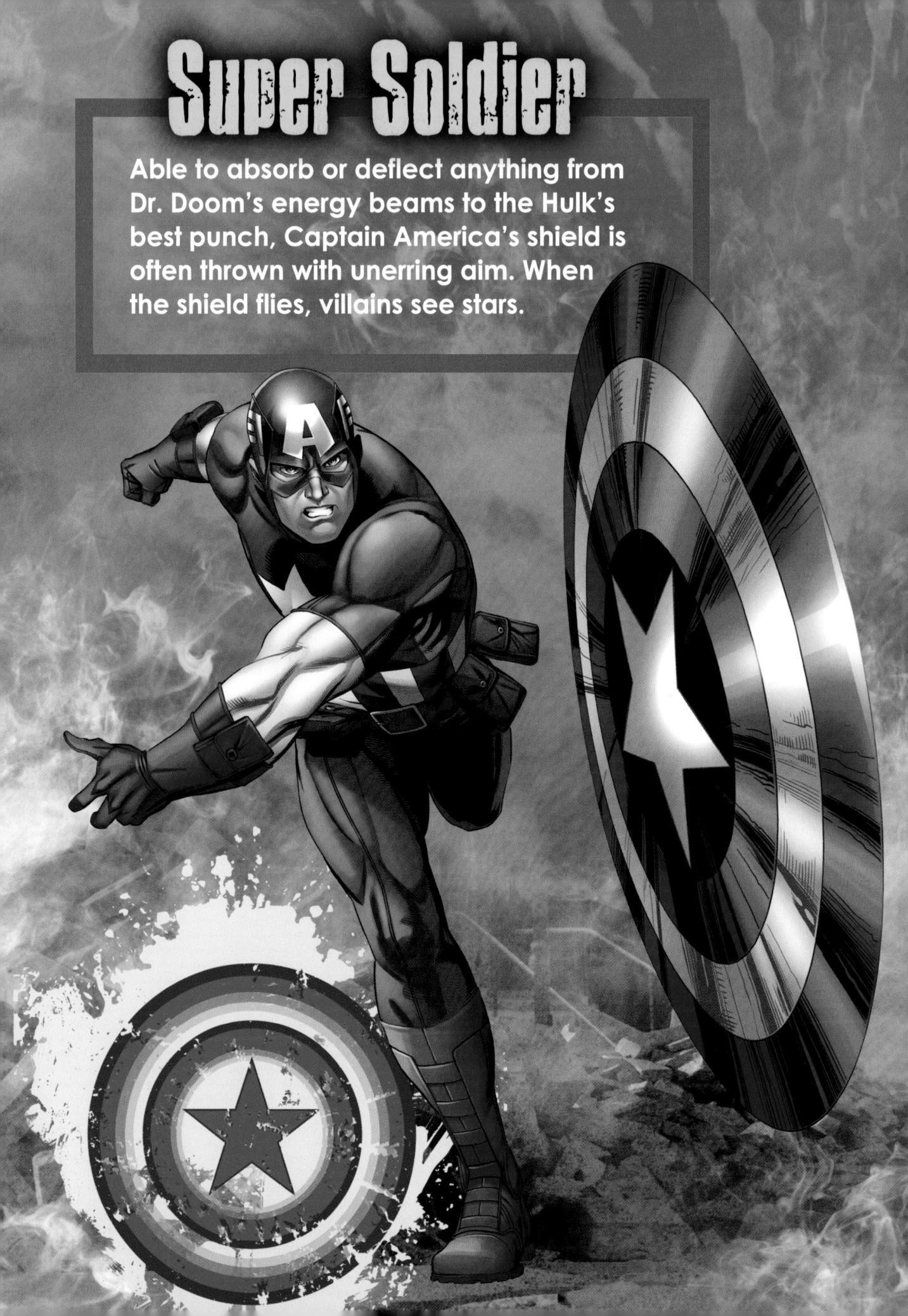

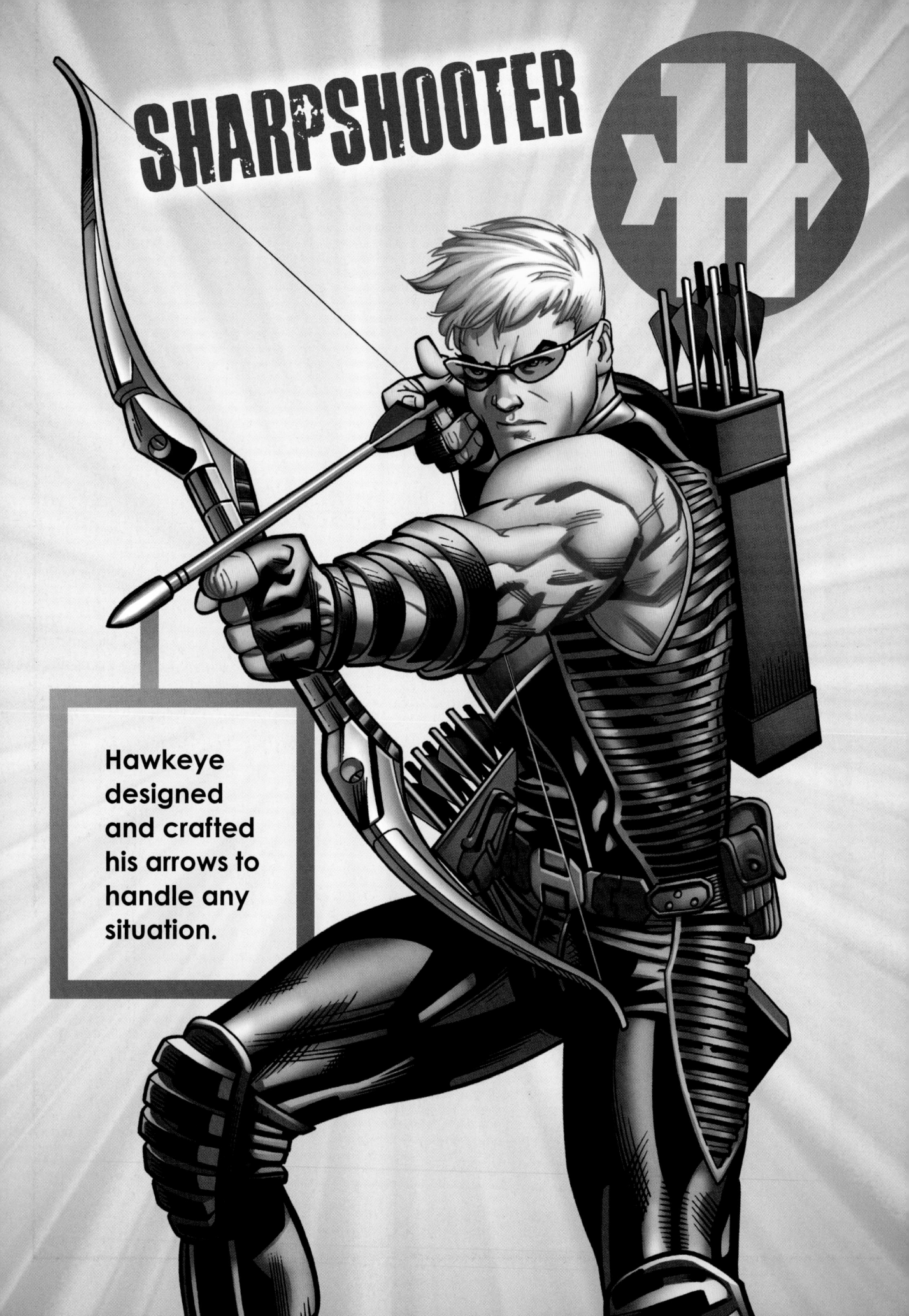

SHARPSHOOTER

Hawkeye designed and crafted his arrows to handle any situation.

HAWKEYE'S TRICK ARROWS HAVE BLINDING FLARES, EXPLOSIVES, ELECTROSHOCKS, KNOCKOUT GAS, SMOKE BOMBS, NETS, GRAPPLING HOOKS, GLUE, BOOMERANGS, AND MORE.

HAWKEYE

SUPERSONIC FLIGHT

Falcon's Feathers:
A Stark Industries
product that rivals
even Iron Man's armor

HOLOGRAPHIC WINGS

Holographic feathers provide supersonic flight and can be fired for explosive effect.

Retractable talons extend for close-range combat.

Widow's Sting

Wrist-mounted electrostatic blasters take down even the toughest enemies.

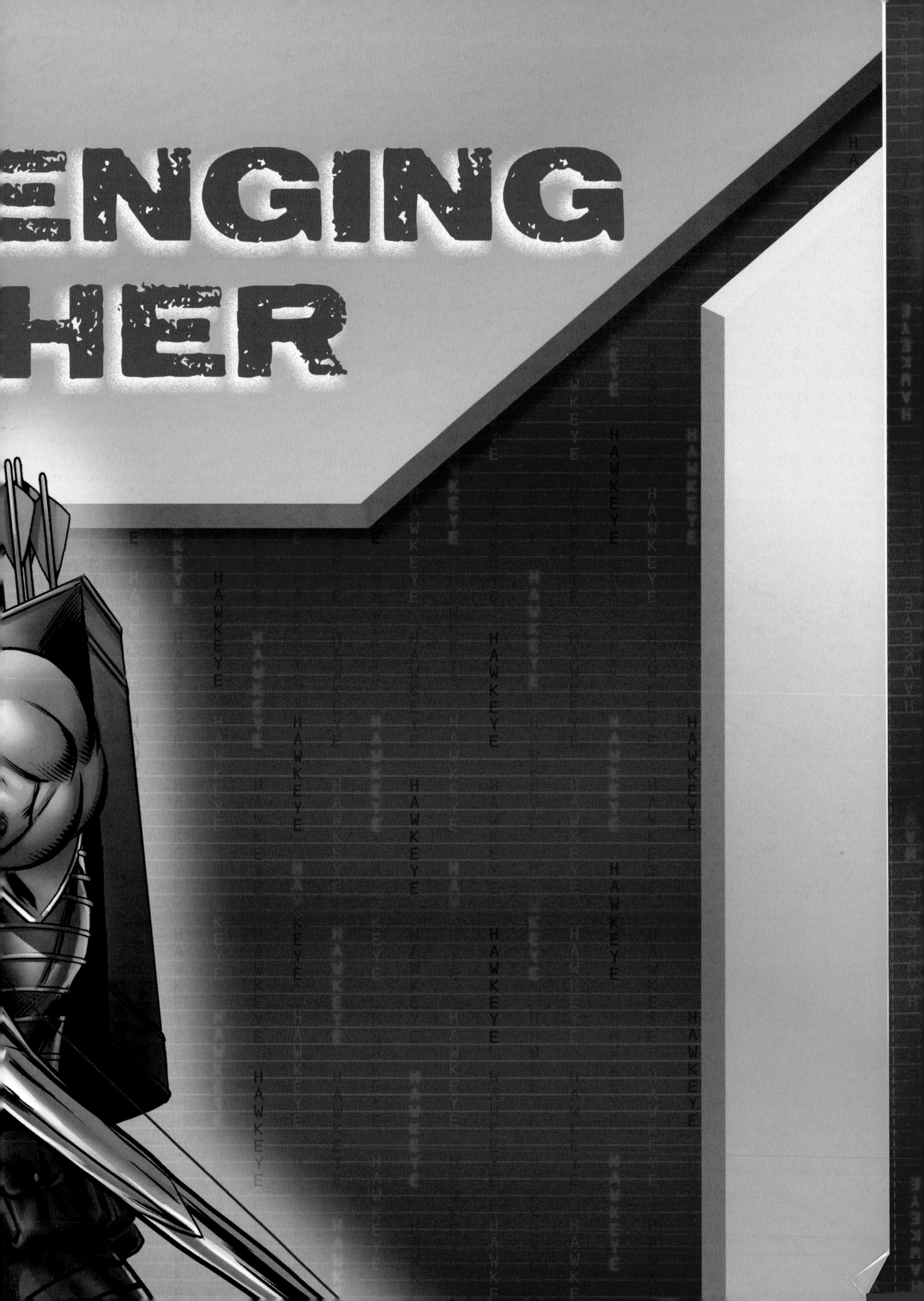
ENGING
HER

BLACK WIDOW'S STING PACKS UP TO 30,000 VOLTS OF PRECISION-AIMED POWER.

TEAMWORK TAKES TIME

Sir, someone has knocked the refrigerator door off its hinges again. Captain America can't figure out the remote. Hawkeye is pouting because someone beat his high score, and I recommend you avoid the bathroom. All I will say is, Hulk was in there last.

I suggest you demonstrate your legendary leadership, sir, and get this team ready for battle.

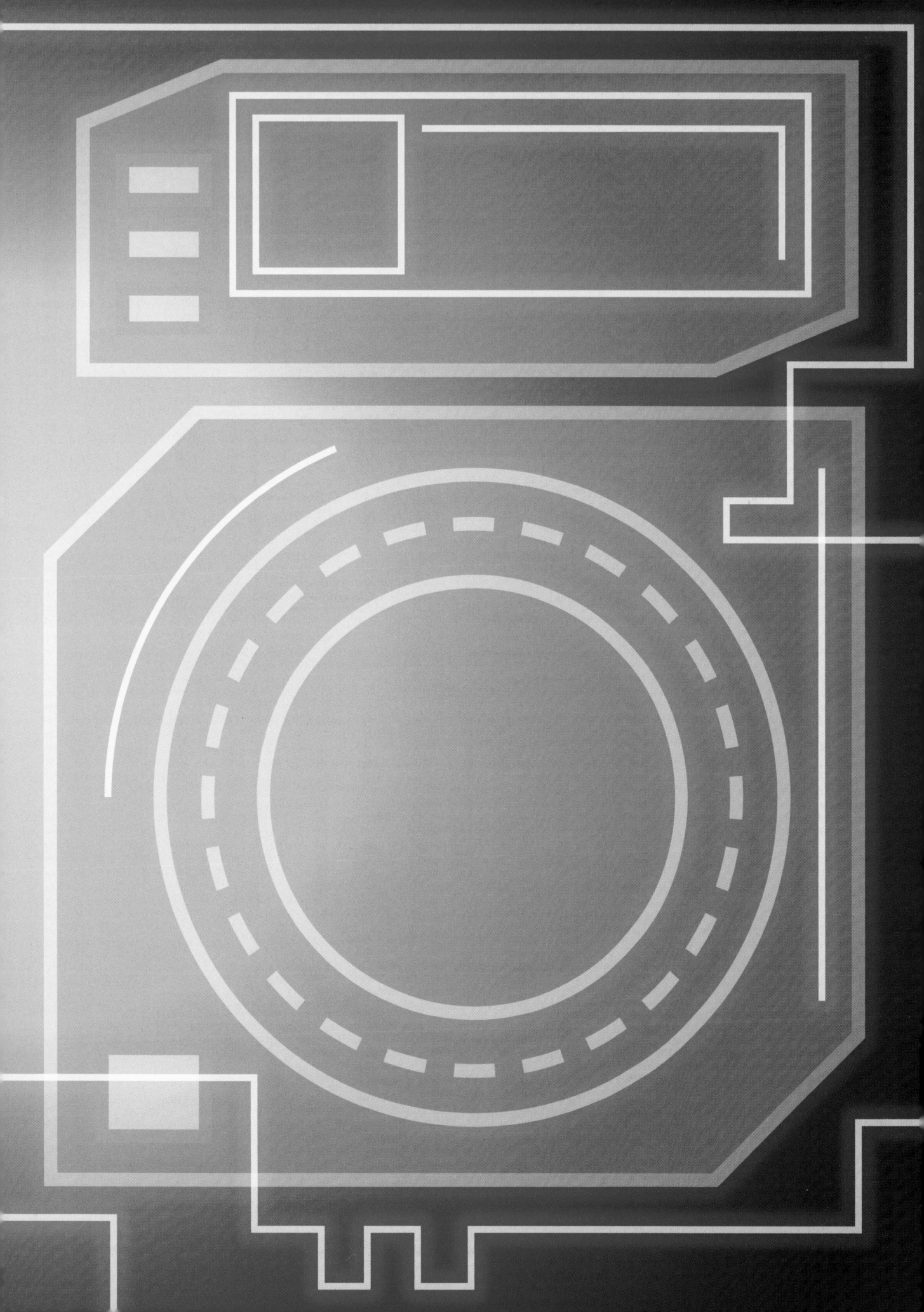

BRAINS OVER BRAWN

EVEN THE BEST LEADERS MAKE MISTAKES.

GOOD OLD-FASHIONED GUTS

UNITED AGAINST A COMMON THREAT!

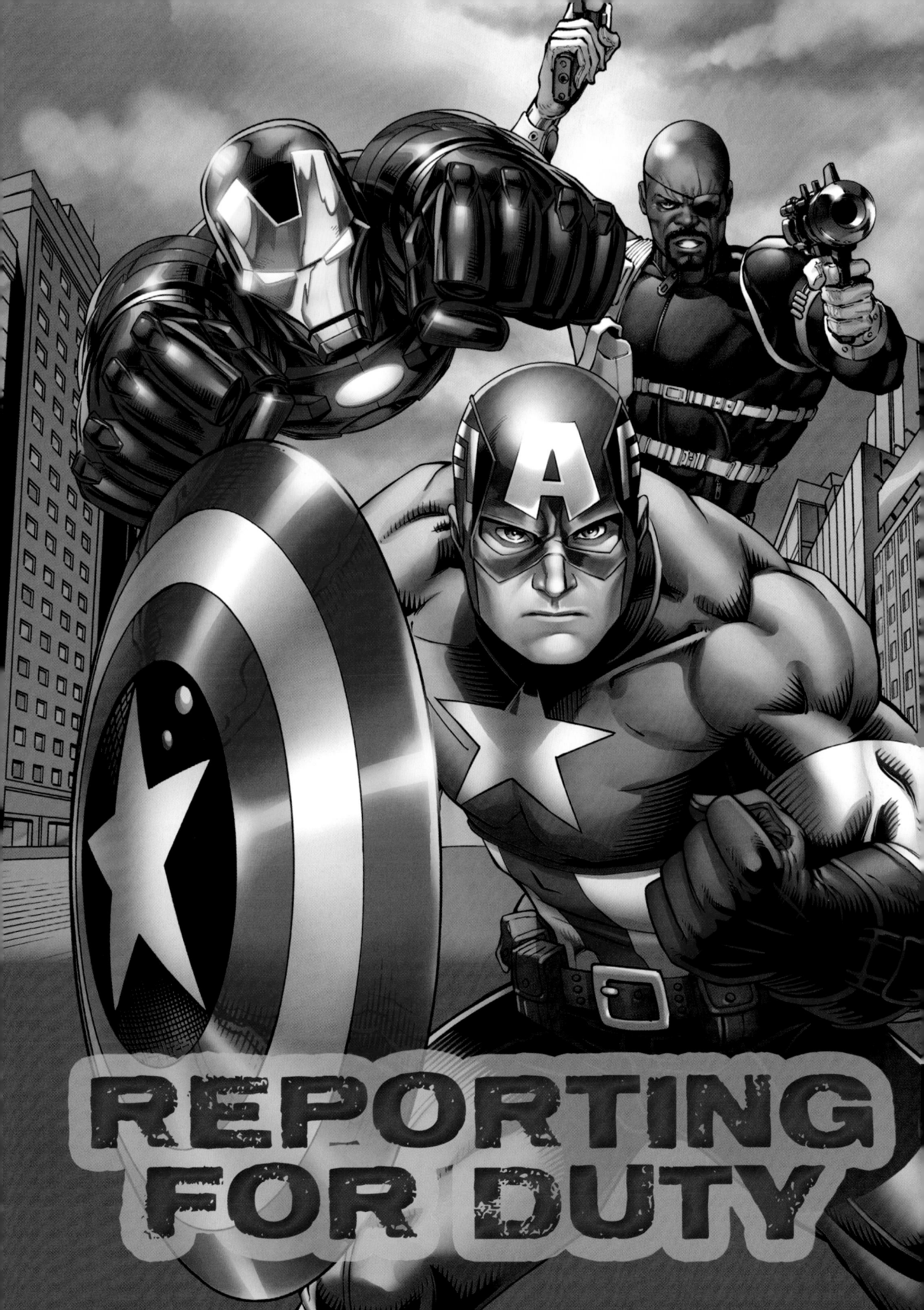

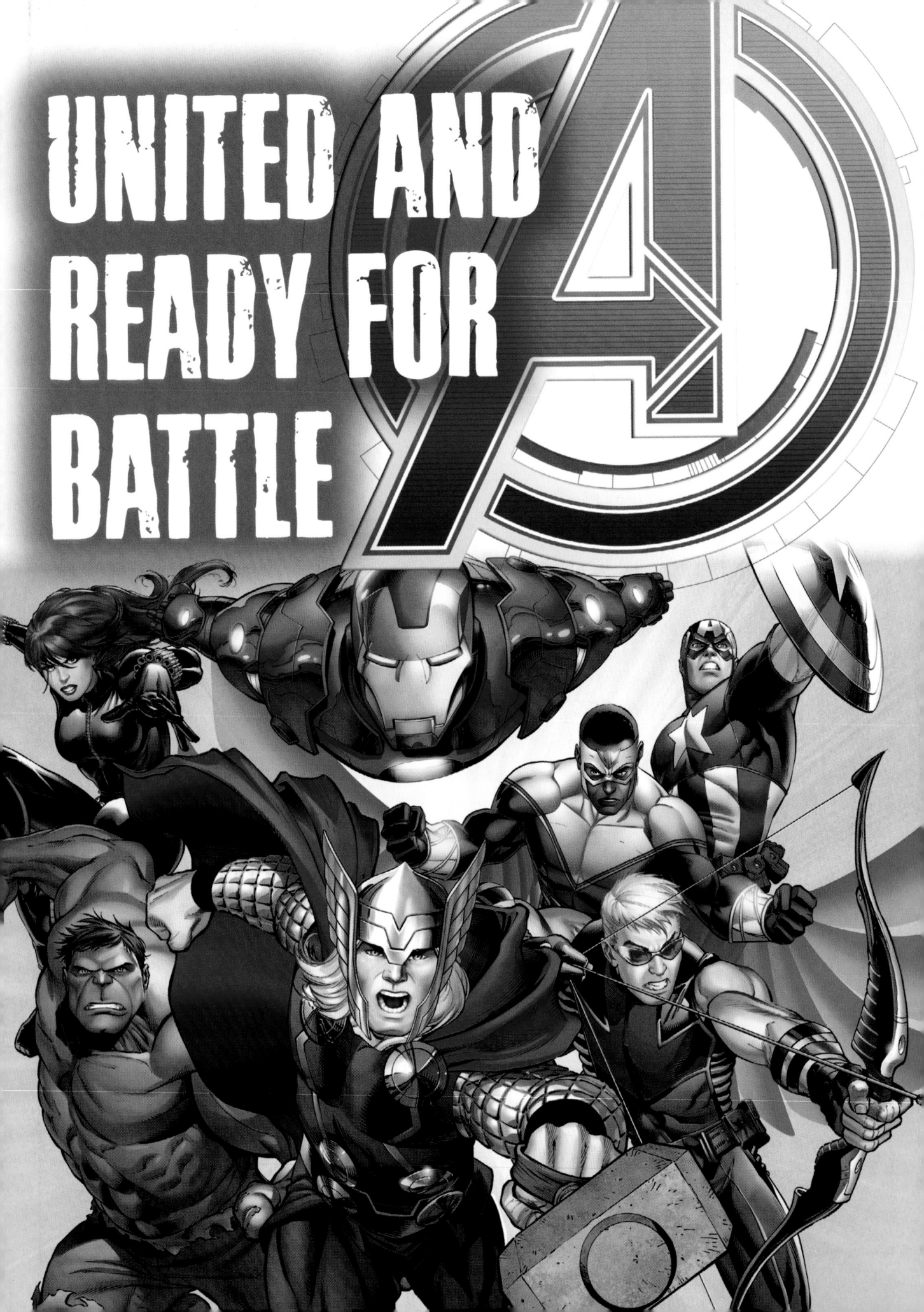

UNITED AND READY FOR BATTLE

IT'S ABOUT GETTING THE JOB DONE.

Fear comes with the job.

It's how you deal with it that matters.

EARTH'S MIGHTIEST HEROES

BRING ON THE BAD GUYS

You're out of time, sir! Our enemies are upon us! S.H.I.E.L.D.'s threat rating is at 10! It's time to find out if you're as good as you think you are!

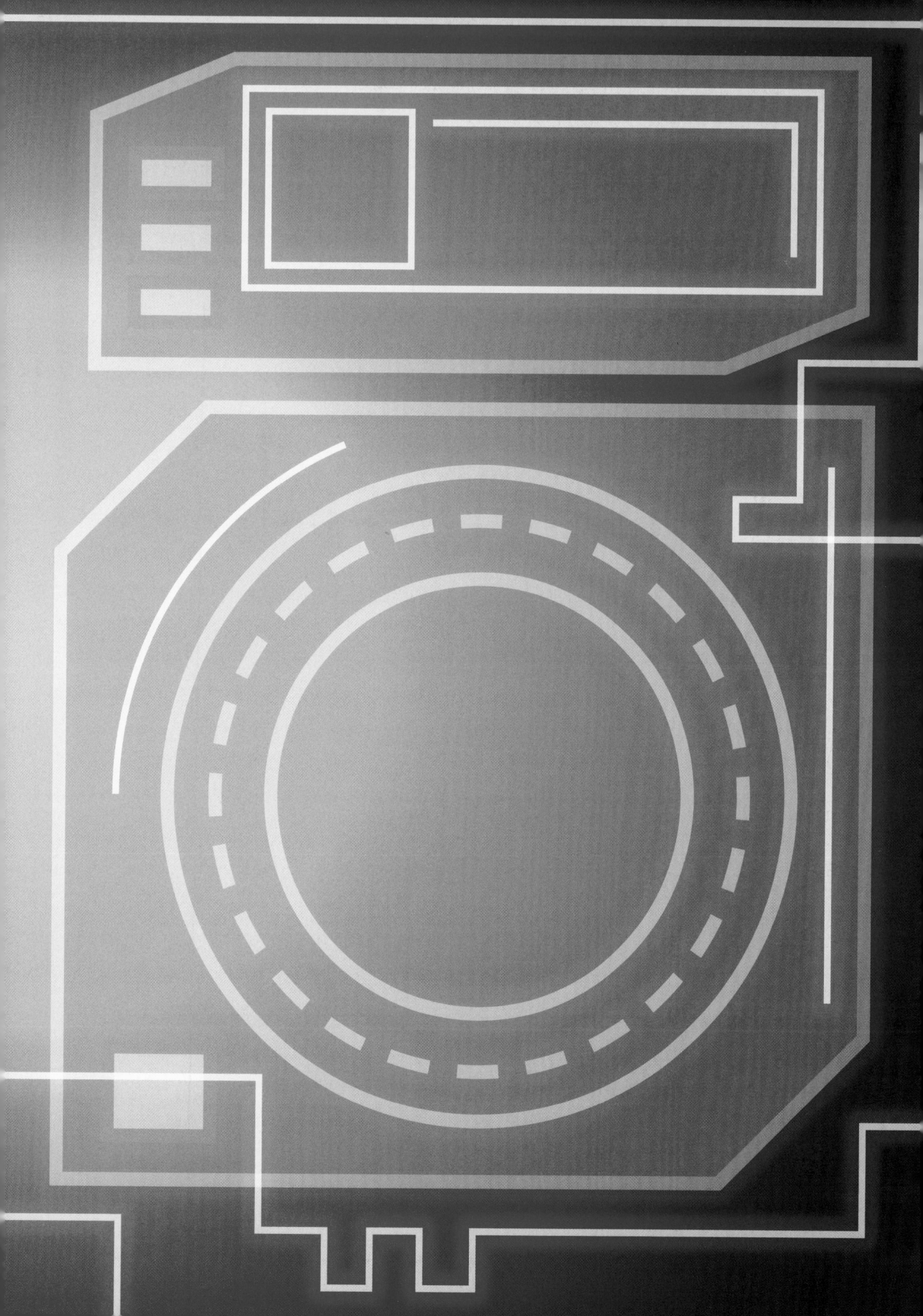

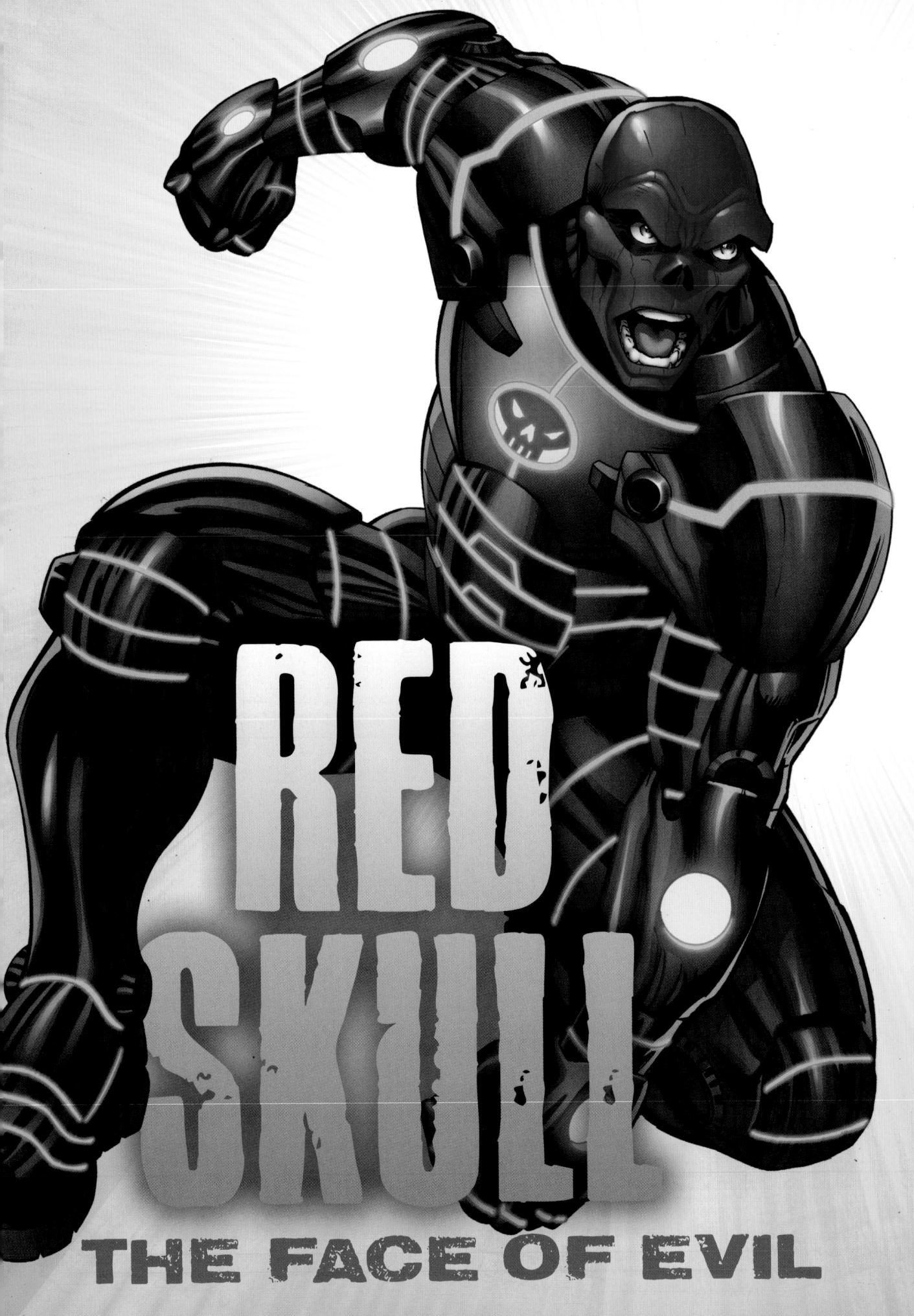

THIS TERRIFYING
TECHNOPATH IS MASTER
OF ALL MACHINES!

SUPER ADAPTOID

TAKES DOWN GODS AND MONSTERS

Super Adaptoid copies your powers, learns your moves, and unleashes them against you. Super Adaptoid knows you better than you know yourself!

ATTUMA

TREMBLE, SURFACE DWELLERS!

WARLORD OF ATLANTIS

The Asgardian trickster god won't be satisfied until he sits on his father Odin's throne . . . and has his brother Thor's head!

ABOMINATION

ABOMINATION WANTS TO SMASH THE HULK. HE HAS THE POWER TO DO IT.

Whiplash built his armor out of hijacked Tony Stark tech. He has energy whips on his hands . . . and a chip on his shoulder.

HYDRA
AGENT

Hydra agents are foot soldiers for Red Skull's assault on liberty. With high-tech armaments hardwired to their nervous systems, Hydra's newest generation is the deadliest yet.

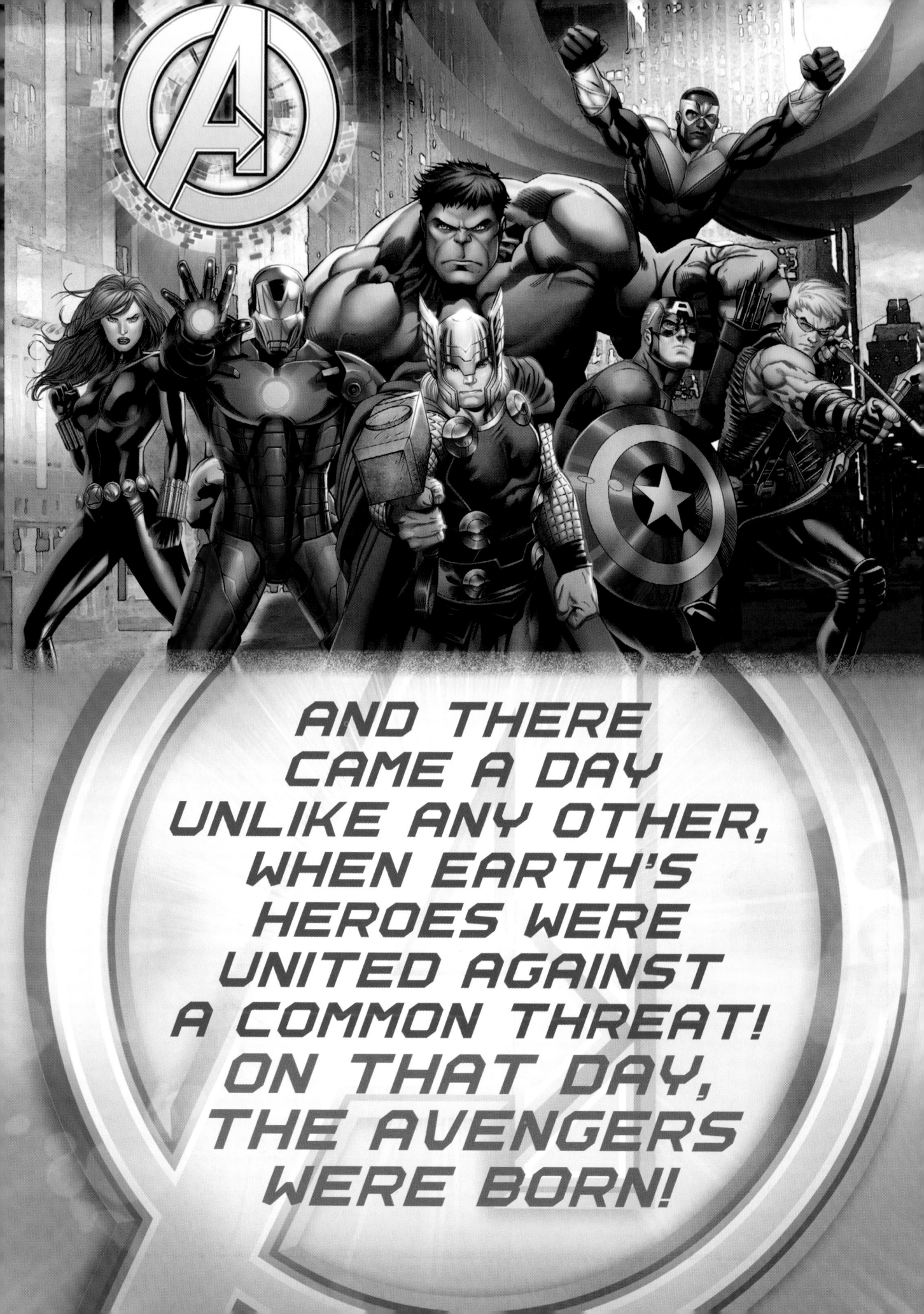

WHAT MAKES A HERO?

Well done, sir! The battle is won! However did you do it? My pre-play simulation calculated the odds of your victory at a mere . . .

Sir? Was that a snore?

Sleep well, sir. It's good to know that if evil rises again, the Avengers will be ready.

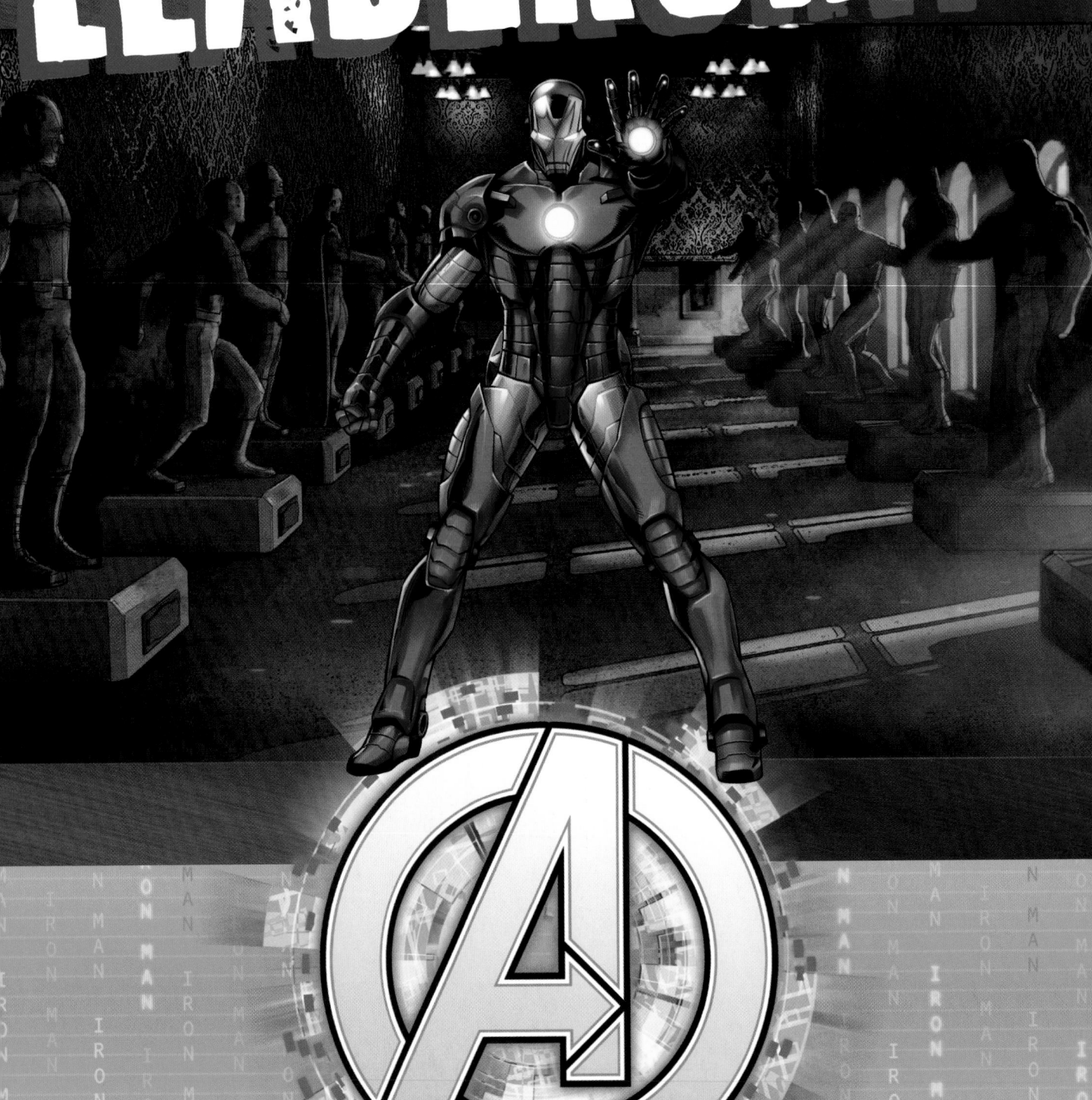

INTEGRITY

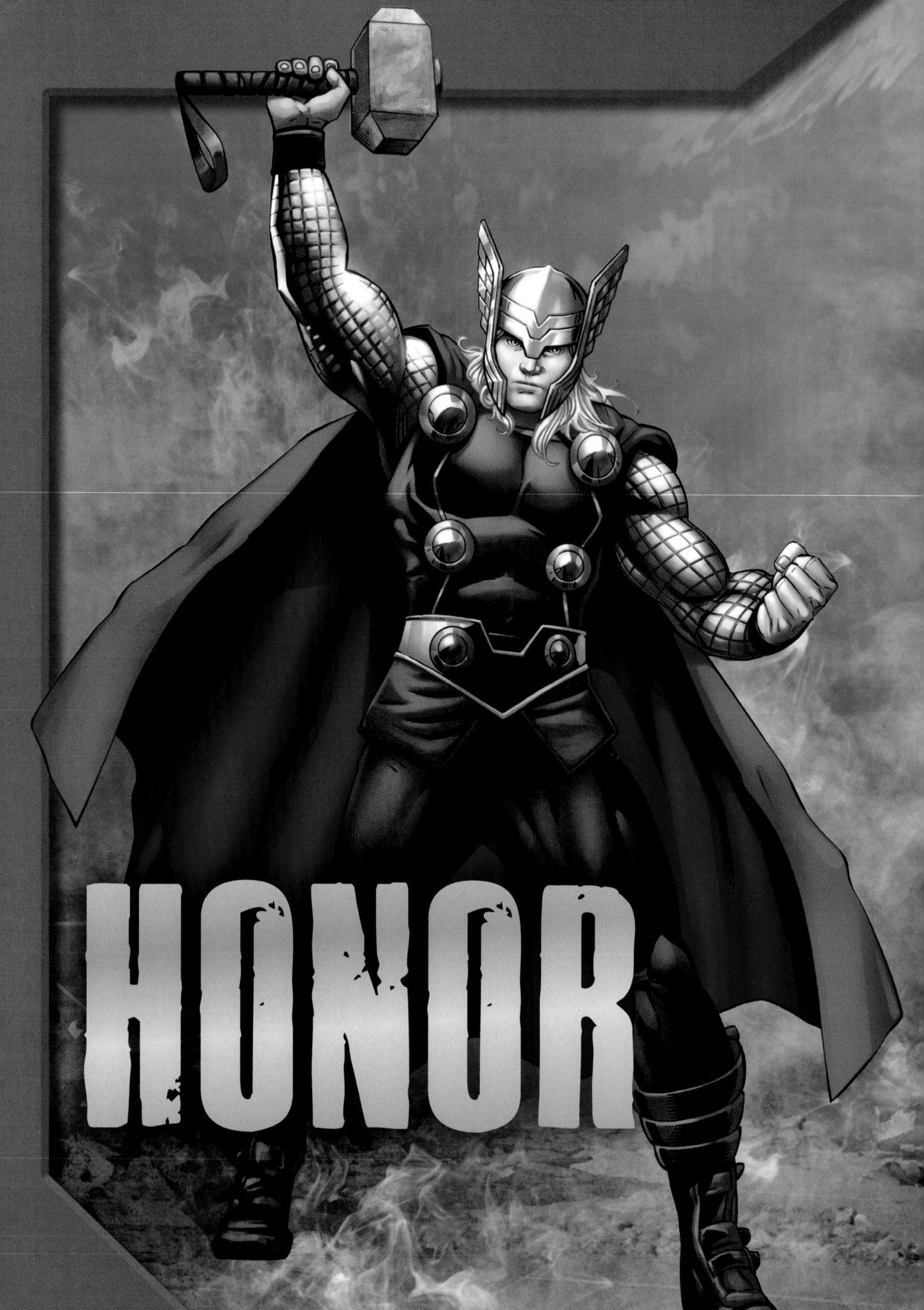

INTELLIGENCE

CONFIDENCE

AVENGERS

SMASH THROUGH EVERY OBSTACLE.

REACH FOR THE
STARS.

UNITED AND READY FOR BATTLE